THE
DIXON
CORNBELT
LEAGUE

W. P. KINSELLA

THE DIXON CORNBELT LEAGUE

and Other Baseball Stories

HarperCollins*Publishers*

The stories in this collection have appeared in an earlier form in the following publications:

"The Baseball Wolf," *Denver Magazine*; "How Manny Embarquadero Overcame and Began His Climb to the Major Leagues," was first published as "Too Good to be True," *Baseball History 4*, Meckler Publishing, 1991; "Searching for January," *Baseball History 3*, Meckler Publishing, 1988; "Feet of Clay," *Iowa City Magazine*, *Spitball*, and *Skybox*; "Lumpy Drobot, Designated Hitter," *Baseball and the Game of Life*, Birch Bark Press, 1990 / Random House, 1991; "The Dixon Cornbelt League," *Editor's Choice III*, The Spirit that Moves Us Press, 1991 and *Baseball History 2*, Meckler Publishing, 1989.

This book was orginally published in Canada in 1993 by HarperCollins Publishers.

HarperCollins books may be purchased for educational, business, or sales promotional use. For information, please write: Special Markets Department, HarperCollins Publishers, Inc., 10 East 53rd Street, New York, NY 10022.

Library of Congress Cataloging-in-Publication Data

Kinsella, W. P.
    The Dixon Cornbelt League and other baseball stories / W. P. Kinsella. —
1st ed.
      p. cm.
    ISBN 0-06-017188-X
    1. Baseball stories, Canadian.   2. Baseball players — Fiction.   I. Title.
[PR9199.3.K443D5   1995]
813'.54 — dc20   94-24653

95 96 97 98 99 RRD 10 9 8 7 6 5 4 3 2 1

For my friends Tony and Elaine Bukoski

CONTENTS

THE
BASEBALL
WOLF

It was during the fifth inning of a game against what translated loosely as the team from no particular location that Denny's Kelly, the shortstop, turned into a wolf.

Denny's Kelly made a diabolically handsome wolf. He was black with streaks of silver, like lightning flashes, along his jowls. There were three silver circles around his bushy tail. One of his paws, which must have each been four inches across, was snow white. Denny's was a very big wolf.

"Shit happens," said Mike Ferrett, the manager, when the change was pointed out to him.

"I think it's more than that," I said.

"How long have you been in Courteguay?" asked Mike Ferrett, not in a kindly tone.

It was a rhetorical question. I had just arrived, had just joined the team. How, I wondered, did a farm boy from northern Michigan end up in a tropical wasteland witnessing the impossible?

"Shouldn't we substitute for him?" I asked.

Since I spoke only English and was the only non-Courteguayan player on the team, I'd been invited to sit beside Ferrett, who was American, though he'd been managing in Courteguay for five years. He spoke English as if his tongue were rusty. His sentences bore a heavy Spanish accent.

I had just been demoted from Triple-A Las Vegas for infractions too numerous to mention, none having to do with my playing ability, all having to do with my not keeping my nose clean, as I had been repeatedly warned to do by management.

The final straw was a rather foolish escapade with the general manager's daughter. I guess most fathers think of their daughters as seven years old. Tanis was twenty-one and most of the things we did, both sexually and with her father's credit cards, were her idea. But would that have been believed? I just stayed silent and accepted responsibility while the general manager arranged to bury me so deep in the organization I'd never be heard from even if I was having a sixty-home-run season and leading the league in stolen bases.

San Barnabas, Courteguay, was the end of the line. The end of the earth. The buck and the trolley and civilization stopped there.

THE
BASEBALL WOLF

As I sat on the bench, I remembered Mike Ferrett's nickname — Rumcake. He had not drawn a sober breath in his final three major-league seasons nor in any of the years he had managed in Courteguay. His face looked as if he had been bobbing for golf balls in a bucket of strawberry jam. He kept a gallon of rum and Coke under the bench. Rumcake Ferrett was connected to the cooler by a length of clear plastic tubing, like an intravenous line.

"Don't expect anybody to learn your name," Ferrett had said to me that afternoon when he picked me up at the airport — two hundred yards of concrete with pampas grass and wild bamboo growing through the cracks. The plane that had brought me from Miami may well have been flown by Amelia Earhart before she disappeared. This time it was piloted by a squat man in a white shirt with turquoise epaulets. Four of the plane's eight seats were occupied, apparently permanently, by soldiers wearing dirty fatigues, carrying weapons, and smoking crooked cigars. "You remember Boo Farnsworth, that old druggie pitcher, flung for the As back in the mid-eighties?"

I nodded.

"Well, he pitched for us until a week ago. Still had good stuff. The drugs had fried everything but his arm — had to be escorted to the mound. I gave the catcher a little whistle and Boo threw toward the sound. Faced the wrong way on the mound at least once an inning. Shortstop'd have to run in and turn him around. Our shortstop's a promising kid, name of Denny's Kelly. His old man played a few years for the White Sox back in the seventies. It seems that when he arrived in America from Courteguay he was so impressed by all the food his meal money would buy that he named his first kid in honor of the restaurant where he always ate, Denny's. When you're a baseball player from Courteguay you don't give a shit about apostrophes.

"Now Boo Farnsworth — a week ago he wandered off to the rain forest to watch the sunrise or something on a couple of pounds of mescaline. He's either dead or he got captured by the insurgents. The government here in Courteguay gets overthrown frequently. If he turns up pitching for the insurgents we'll know he's alive. Otherwise, he'll go on the big disabled list in the sky. Missing in action.

"I speak the lingo here, so I'm not considered a genuine foreigner," said Ferrett, taking a long pull from a Coke bottle well fortified with rum. "You, though, will be called Gringo Uno. That was what Boo was called. We've never had more than one foreigner on the squad. I suppose if we did he'd be Gringo Dos. Things are a little out of focus here in Courteguay.

"So, Gringo Uno, you want to tell me what you did to get exiled here?"

"I prefer not to."

"Anything I should know of? You have fits? Carry a gun in your jockstrap? You got a penchant for kids under six?"

"None of the above," I said.

Ferrett scratched his head, took another pull from the Coke bottle. "Just don't surprise me. I don't like surprises."

"Would you classify this as a surprise?" I asked Ferrett, nodding toward where Denny's sat on his haunches at shortstop, grinning his large wolf grin and salivating amiably on the yellow dust of the infield.

Before the game I'd watched Denny's work out. He showed amazing agility, an iron arm, and a unselfconscious congeniality with players and fans alike, aided by a smile that could ripen oranges and turn young girls' knees to jelly.

"Shit happens," Ferrett repeated. "Welcome to Courteguay."

I had heard more than rumors about the weird goings-on in Courteguay. At my going-away party my teammates told stories about people turned into butterfly-covered statues, a Baseball Hall of Famer on display in a crystal coffin at the capitol building, flowers with lives of their own, and, of course, the famous Cortizar twins, Julio and Esteban, who began their baseball careers as pitcher and catcher inside their mother's womb. So a wolf playing shortstop did not strike me as all that unusual.

"How's he gonna turn the pivot on a double play?" I asked Ferrett. "You've got to take him out."

Ferrett took a pull on the plastic line that must have lowered the contents of the cooler by a quart.

"Has this happened before?" I asked.

Ferrett remained silent. The player beside me said, "Sí. El lobo."

"I thought you said no one else on the team except Denny's speaks English," I said to Ferrett.

"Did you hear anybody speak English?" said Ferrett, sending signs to his third-base coach.

Courteguay is shaped like the moon on a small finger nail and is not much larger. It manages to border both Haiti and the Dominican Republic, its residents speaking slightly more Spanish than French. Its official language, I've been told, is baseball. For its size Courteguay produces more major-league baseball players than any country in the world. There are rumors that somewhere in the jungle there is a genetic-engineering factory — or maybe a coven of voodoo aficionados — that produces iron-armed stortstops and lithe, home-run-hitting outfielders. I considered such things to be rumors until I watched Denny's Kelly turn into a wolf.

"Shit happens," said Ferrett. "Though more often in Courteguay than anywhere else. My theory is, if it doesn't upset the locals, it doesn't upset me. That attitude and a quart of rum a day make living in Courteguay passable. Or possible. Or both."

Ferrett had explained to me earlier that the opposition team had been breathed out of the jungle just before game time. They were given political amnesty for the evening.

"They're insurgents of some kind. Last year they were the government. I think there's about to be a revolution again. Probably the tenth since I've been here."

Our team, the San Barnabas Angels, sported virgin-white uniforms with turquoise numbers and letters. Our opponents wore military camouflage, their only distinguishing marks red armbands. Their rifles leaned against the wall of their dugout with the bats.

"Win or lose they get a fifteen-minute head start after the game is officially over," said Ferrett. "Tomorrow every one of them will shoot your ears off if they get the chance."

No one seemed particularly alarmed when Denny's Kelly turned into a wolf. There was a runner on first and two out at the time. The next batter hit a high bouncer between short and second. Denny's moved gracefully to his left, leapt several feet in the air like a dog after a Frisbee, and accepted the ball in his huge jaws. After he landed he loped across second base for the force-out, well ahead of the advancing runner.

"El lobo," whispered the second stringers, up and down the bench.

Denny's raced off the field with his fellow players, tail wagging, and took his usual seat on the bench between the third baseman and the center-fielder. They did not seem alarmed. He was panting extravagantly, I assumed to cool himself, for the temperature must have been a hundred degrees, the humidity at least as high. His gums were black, his tongue pink and black, his teeth long and ivory-colored.

"How's he going to bat?" I asked Ferrett.

"Son, if he wants to bat, I don't plan to stop him. Do you?"

At bat, Denny's stood more or less upright, held the bat in his mouth, guided it with his white paw. He laid down a lovely bunt, raced for first like a splash of muddy water, beating the throw by two strides. He stole second without drawing a throw, but was stranded when the next batter struck out.

As we were preparing to leave the clubhouse, Ferrett said, "There's been a small change of plans."

"Exactly what sort of change?"

I'd noticed that immediately after the game the Courteguayan players had held a hurried meeting in the corner of the locker room. Ferrett still had my bags in his stationwagon. It was team policy, he said, that all players, even the one or two natives of San Barnabas, stayed at a team hotel. He had promised to drop me off after the game. He had even introduced me to my roommate at the ballpark, a tall relief pitcher with thin, thoroughbred legs, named Pasqual something-something.

"Pasqual here is interested in learning conversational English," Ferrett had said.

Pasqual's eyes looked like fried eggs, huge whites, brown yolks.

"*Gringo Uno*, charmed I'm certain," said Pasqual, smiling crookedly.

"I . . . am . . . pleased . . . to . . . meet . . . you," I said, enunciating each word clearly.

"California . . . electric . . . appliance," said Pasqual, also enunciating clearly.

"Me too," I said.

During the team meeting I had heard the words *Gringo Uno* bandied about frequently.

"You're going to room with Denny's instead of Pasqual," said Ferrett. He was carrying his cooler of rum and Coke by its handle, the way a plumber might carry his toolbox. The plastic line peeked from the buttonhole in the lapel of his jacket, easily accessible if he bent his head down and to the left.

"Shit happens," I said, assuming my originality of speech would impress Ferrett.

"Damned superstitious lot, these Courteguayans," he said.

"The wolf's not likely to kill me for a midnight snack, is he?"

Ferrett didn't answer.

When I found Room 7, on the ground floor of a long, swaybacked three-story frame building, there were two small suitcases propped against the door. They did not belong to me. Denny's was sitting on his haunches staring at the doorknob. When he saw me he sniffed the two suitcases and smiled.

"I assume you don't have a key?" I said.

"Rowl," said Denny's.

"With paws like that you probably have a little trouble with the principle of the doorknob," I said. "But I understand wolf scientists are working on it. When the breakthrough comes it will open a lot of doors for wolfkind."

"Rowl," said Denny's.

"That was a joke," I said.

Inside, Denny's walked the perimeter of the room, sniffing, marking his territory.

"You realize it's going to smell like wolf piss in here," I said. "When you have more serious bodily functions to attend to I'd appreciate it if you'd use the john. *Comprendez?*"

"Rowl," said Denny's.

We watched television for a while. I *Love Lucy* in Spanish. Denny's barked when Lucy spilled a platter of pork chops on Fred Mertz. The bark sounded like LUNCH! We watched the news in pidgin something-or-other. I was able to pick up an English word or two, enough to understand the major-league scores. *El Cincinnati, dos, San Francisco, uno.* I suspect Denny's, who lay on the bed with his nose on his extended front paws, got more out of it than I did. My Spanish was limited to *huevos rancheros* and a few other menu items.

"Is it true wolves are color blind?" I asked during a commercial.

"Rowl," said Denny's.

THE
BASEBALL WOLF

We eventually went to sleep. Denny's curled up on the floor, turning in three tight circles before he did so. Once, I peered over the side of the bed; a bright yellow eye was trained on me like a searchlight. I like to sleep on my stomach with my right arm hanging off the edge. I tucked my arm carefully under my body before I went to sleep.

I was wakened by the sound of Denny's toenails clicking on the cracked and dirty linoleum. I turned slowly toward the sound. Denny's was stretching upward, placing his large paws on the middle sash of the window, his body blocking most of the moonlight from the room, leaving a huge black wolf silhouette between me and the outside world. Then he howled, his large, wet nose pointing straight up, his eyes glimmering in the moonlight. The sound vibrated the window glass, full of pain and longing, soaring out over half the landlocked republic.

Through the thin walls of what Ferrett referred to as the Roach Motel I heard a dozen sleep-choked voices muttering, "*El lobo, el lobo.*"

Someone banged down a window. Directly above us someone whacked on the floor with a shoe.

Denny's howled again. The loneliness was palpable.

I slowly sat up, bracing myself on one elbow.

"Is there anything I can do?" I asked.

Denny's snuffled at the windowpane, whining excitedly, his breath sending dust and dead flies floating to the floor. It sounded like, "Give me a minute."

And a minute was about what it took for the tall wolf to change back into a man.

"Sorry if I've frightened you," Denny's said, turning from the window. "You've been very tolerant. And, yes, wolves see the world in black and white."

He spoke English with only a slight Spanish accent. He was a husky young man, with skin the color of black lacquer. His eyes glowed white as fish bellies.

"I spent my first ten years in the United States," he went on. "My father played in Chicago, and later for the California Angels."

"I see," I said. "May I ask about the wolf?"

"It would be better if you didn't."

I nodded. "Do you want to get some sleep?" I said, moving to my edge of the bed.

"Actually, I'm very hungry," said Denny's. "I usually eat after the game. Do you want to go out and get some food? I know of a good all-night café."

I was already pulling on my socks.

"What I wanted when I howled was for you to open the window. I wanted to go hunting. I was very hungry. It's odd, but my thoughts remain confused for a while after I change. When I was suggesting the café I was thinking of ordering a field mouse or two. They're actually quite delicious, though chickens are better. Pheasant tastes best, but they're difficult to capture."

We walked through the midnight streets of San Barnabas, to a small, smoky café. Denny's ordered us something with tortillas and eggs, salsa and white cheese. The coffee was strong enough to melt brick.

"I'm sorry, but I'm going to ask some questions," I said. "Does turning into a wolf have anything to do with geography? With this being Courteguay? Did someone turn you into a wolf? Is it like a curse? Could it happen to me?"

"To deal with the last first, only if you so desired."

"I could be a wolf if I wanted to?"

"You could be whatever beast is within."

I thought about that for a moment. What beast is within? Do I have a choice? If I did have a choice, what beast would I be?

"How do I know what's within?" I asked. What if my beast turned out to be an armadillo, I wondered irrationally. I had an uncle in Longview, Texas, who claimed to have been a Roadkill Disposal Engineer for the Texas Department of Highways. His job was scraping dead armadillos off Texas highways.

On our way back to the Roach Motel, Denny's said, "You either know or you don't know. If you don't know, nothing special will happen to you. Most people don't know."

We walked in silence. The humidity made the air so thick I could feel the fungus growing. I tried to run the high points of my life by my inner vision.

Suddenly I found myself telling Denny's about my northern Michigan childhood, about the great horned owls.

*   *   *

The great horned owls would sit on the highest l
es of a dead sycamore, sometimes there'd be two
there were three, their horned shapes dark agains
moon, the pale branches of the tree glowing like fo\
their eyes yellow lanterns.

My father and I would lie down on the far edge of
the meadow and take turns watching the owls through
binoculars. Our eyes would grow accustomed to the
night, the star-infested sky, the gold coin of moon
reflecting eerie blues and pale yellows.

Eventually the owls, one by one, would take flight, the
muffled flapping of their wings like gentle drum beats.
They would loom dark against the sky, casting black
shadows. Sometimes we could see the moon glance off
their unfurled talons. We would watch an owl glide
silently toward the earth, pull up a hair's breadth short of
contact, rise with an ominous flapping of wings, a
mouse or other nocturnal creature clutched in its claws.

It was such a thrill to witness the owls, stolid as statues, clinging to the dead tree limbs the color of their
feathers, to hear their gentle but frightening hoots like
notes from an oboe, the grace of their flight, the delicacy of their attack, the simplicity with which they
brought death to their prey.

"That's what I want to be," I said to Denny's, when I'd
finished my story.

"If that is your beast within," he said enigmatically. "You cannot yet imagine the thrill of transformation. The heightened senses, like being covered with tingling electrical pulses. And the chill of instinct, pure and bright as blood . . ."

"When can I do it?" My veins felt like they were pulsating with neon.

"Sleep on it," Denny's said.

Soon we were back in the stifling room.

"It smells like wolf piss in here," Denny's said, smiling a smile so dangerous young girls would faint, as he flopped down on his side of the bed.

Denny's the baseball player remained with us all the next day. We played the team from no particular location and won in a walkover, fourteen to one. Ferrett drank himself to sleep by the sixth inning. The third-base coach did what little managing was necessary. I got to play left field and went four for six with two doubles and three RBIs. Denny's played flawlessly at shortstop, had three hits and two stolen bases.

After the game we ate at the café and went back to our room tired and happy.

"Be patient," Denny's said after the light was out. "What is meant to be will happen."

I could see his white semicircle of smile.

I wakened in the middle of the night.

Denny's was staring out the window.

"It can be done," he said, when he saw that I was awake, "if you want it badly enough. Concentrate. See yourself as the owl. Stare at the moon, let your eyes go white. Will yourself to become what you want most and it will happen."

"I believe you," I said.

"Then the hardest part is over."

"Is it because this is Courteguay?" I asked. But Denny's did not answer. His hands, braced on the middle window sash, were already turning into paws. His face was rearranging itself as a cloud blew across the golden moon, becoming long and lantern-jawed. *Lupine* I believe is the word.

A moment later he howled, a sound encompassing all the aloneness of the wilderness. Windows slammed shut. Whispers of "*El lobo*" reverberated through the old hotel.

I walked around the bed, turned the paint-stiffened lock in the center of the sash, eased Denny's back from the window, and forced the window up until it was wide open. I let go gingerly, prepared for it to slam down, but it did not. The window was not used to being opened. It stuck tightly.

"We'll be able to come back without creating insult in the lobby," I said.

"Rowl," said Denny's.

He placed his front paws on the sill, stuck his head out, and looked both ways, as if preparing to cross a street. I could see his back legs tightening, preparing to launch him the few feet to the parking lot.

"Wait for me," I said.

Denny's turned and stared, a questioning look in his burning amber eyes.

"I'm going to try," I said. "I want this very badly."

Denny's waited.

I sat cross-legged on the bed. I locked my fingers together, my thumbs tight against my chest. I closed my eyes and pictured snow, a few leafy flakes drifting down like white postage stamps from a cloud that did not yet cover the iridescent peach that was the October moon. A frosty night, the brown grasses of the meadow tipped white, my father and I in parkas, wrapped in blankets, me with a Thermos of hot chocolate, Dad drinking coffee laced with Irish whiskey. A tufted great horned owl, its feathers already winter-white, sits on a ghostly branch of a dead tree. We watch. We wait. The bird's large eyes tunnel yellow light in our direction. We become part of the landscape.

The feathery edge of a cloud slides like smoke across the glittering moon. My hearing is acute, beyond anything I've ever experienced; I can hear a leaf rattling on an aspen yards into the forest. I can hear something small scampering through the grasses at the edge of the meadow.

My bones are hollow. I feel myself shrinking, light as air, strong as steel. Hunger and watchfulness.

I am perched on the sill beside Denny's. My eyes pierce the night. Though Denny's makes no sound, I know he has told me it is time to go. He tenses, leaps from the window, lands soundlessly on the dark pads of his feet in the asphalt parking lot.

I tense, spread my wings, and, with the muffled sound of a flannel sheet in the wind, launch myself into the ink-blue, tropical night. Denny's lopes along while my wings flap gently high above him.

My entrails hum with hunger.

"The ballpark," Denny's is saying, though all he has done is growl softly.

We pass a couple of drunken men near the café.

"El lobo," they say in slurred, wondering voices.

They do not see me above them.

Outside the ballpark, Denny's digs with urgency until he clears enough space to crawl under the outfield fence.

I circle high in the silvered sky until I glimpse my moonshadow. An owl in the outfield. I picture the high white sky of day, drifting lazily, hurtling suddenly downward toward a baseball struck toward the sky.

Denny's lopes across the outfield grass, his footprints standing out magically, as if embossed on the damp grass. He sniffs along the outfield fence. I can hear his breath as if he is next to me. I hear the terrified squeak of the mouse he snatches from its hiding place. I smell the warm odor of blood.

THE
BASEBALL WOLF

Thirty yards down the fence, toward the left-field corner, I spot a kangaroo rat. It picks up something in its dainty paws, its nose trembles, its BB eyes dart. I turn a lazy circle, then launch myself in a steep dive. I can smell its fear. As I slash through the hot night air, I feel my pearly talons unfurl.

THE
FADEAWAY

I t is the top of the eighth in the year 2000. Tag Murtagh is in his third precarious season as manager of the Cleveland Indians. They have been contenders ever since he took them over. Five and a half games out in '98, four and a half in '99. Now, just after the All-Star break, they are only two games behind the Yankees, and hosting them in the first of a four-game series.

The Yankees have two on and one out, and Murtagh's starting pitcher, Babe Crater, is in trouble. The guy with the radar gun directly behind home plate holds up five fingers — Crater's last fastball had lost five miles per hour from his velocity at the start of the game.

Murtagh doesn't have a certified closer. Cleveland has the worst bullpen in the American League, with an ERA of 5.32 in their last twenty games.

"How about the rumors you're gonna trade one of your big hitters for a quality reliever?" the Sporting News had asked Murtagh just before the game.

"I'm only the manager," he replied. "I don't make the deals, but I hate having to leave my starters in until their arms are limp as dicks leaving a whorehouse. Any deal to get us a quality reliever would be welcomed with open arms by this manager."

Murtagh glances down the roster, his hand tentatively reaching for the phone to the bullpen. This month's closer is a wild-eyed Panamanian named Fernando Gozer. He is as likely to throw his ninety-eight-mile-an-hour fastball behind the hitter or twenty feet up the screen as in the vicinity of the plate. Murtagh's set-up man is Rick Robinson, a pitcher as nondescript as his name. He is in his fifteenth season in the Bigs and survives on guile alone. Both are warmed up and ready.

Reluctantly deciding on Robinson, Murtagh reaches for the bullpen phone.

"Yes," says a voice he can't immediately place. Usually bullpen coach Bert Path answers with a mumbled "Yeah?"

"Robinson," he says.

"If I might make a suggestion, Ed Jerusalem would be a better choice."

"Who the hell is this?"

"Crater has suffered a minor muscle pull, though he'll be reluctant to admit it. I suggest you go to the mound, force the issue, and then go to the umpire. As Crater is injured, Jerusalem will be given all the time he needs to warm up."

"Who the hell is this? Jerusalem, is that you? Put Bert on right now."

Murtagh knows Ed Jerusalem can't say three words without cursing. He is a 230-pound hulk with a drooping mustache and a pound of tobacco in his cheek. He is whale shit (where does that term come from, Murtagh wonders?), the eleventh pitcher, the guy you bring in in the fourth inning when you're behind nine to nothing. His job is to suffer whatever indignities are in store to give the real pitching staff a rest.

Jerusalem had once been an average starter — he had a .500 record with three different clubs — then was a passable middle reliever and occasional closer for second division teams. But he is thirty-three years old and, like the rest of the Cleveland bullpen, ineffective most of the time, just an aging body filling up space on the roster until some minor leaguer matures.

But Bert Path doesn't come to the phone. Murtagh signals the pitching coach to go out and talk to the pitcher.

"Kill some time, Griff," he rasps. "Ask the SOB if he's injured. Phone's all fucked up."

"Put Bert on," he shouts into the phone.

"Bert isn't available at the moment," the cultured voice replies. "I strongly suggest you use Ed Jerusalem."

Murtagh slams down the phone.

"Mutt," he says to his bench coach, "get the hell down to the bullpen and see who's fucking with the phone."

The umpire is making his way to the mound. Griff Wilson, the pitching coach, has stalled as long as possible. He exchanges a few words with the umpire, turns and makes his way toward the dugout so slowly that his progress is almost imperceptible. The fans boo good-naturedly. Griff's nickname is Snail.

The bullpen phone jangles.

"Everybody's warmed up and waiting," Mutt Rodriguez drawls. He is a tenth-generation Georgian who speaks only English. "They say nobody's been near the phone, and that it ain't rung."

"Like hell," says Murtagh. "What's Jerusalem doing?"

"Jerusalem?"

"Yeah. What the fuck's he doing?"

"Ed ain't figurin' on pitching today. He using them infra-red binoculars of his to shoot a little beaver up in the left-field bleachers."

"He hasn't been near the phone?"

"Jerusalem don't even know what day it is unless you tell him. All he's interested in is fatty foods and blond pussy. Bert swears nobody's touched the phone. There must be a short circuit or something."

"Shit! When I get whoever's been fucking with me there's gonna be hell to pay. Send in Robinson."

Murtagh slams down the phone and heads for the mound, where his pitcher has been stalling, pointlessly

throwing to first base even though the base runner is
not a threat to steal, and has only a two-step lead.

Robinson's second pitch is slashed into the right field
corner, scoring the tying run. Because the runner on
first runs slower than water finding its own level, he is
held at third. The next batter flies to deep center and the
Yankees take the lead. They add an insurance run in the
ninth and Cleveland loses another game they would have
won if they had a competent bullpen.

After Murtagh clears away the media, making the usual
flimsy excuses for his feeble bullpen, he closes the door
to his office and waits until the stadium is quiet. Murtagh
likes this time of day best, late evening, virtually alone in
a complex that often holds sixty thousand people.

Murtagh makes his way through the echoing concrete
tunnels out to the dugout. The field is dark, the stands
dimly lighted where a few cleaners sweep and gather.
He sits on the bench and stares at the bullpen phone.

He lifts the yellow receiver, hears the distant ring of
the bullpen phone way out behind the left-field fence.

The phone clicks.

"Good evening," says the voice.

"Who the hell is this?"

"My advice was to use Ed Jerusalem this evening."

"Why should I take your advice?"

"Because of my experience as a pitcher. I have some
knowledge of baseball and pitching."

"So does half the population of America — just enough to be dangerous. What makes you any different?"

"Christy Mathewson."

"What about him?"

"You're talking to him."

"Shit! What, are you crazy?"

"No, but I am Christy Mathewson."

"Haven't you been dead for about fifty years?"

"It will be seventy-five years in October."

"Congratulations."

"I had 373 wins, 26 of them as a reliever. I had 27 saves in an era when saves weren't considered a pertinent statistic. I believe I'm qualified to talk about pitching. Ed Jerusalem has the potential to be another Dennis Eckersley."

"Bert? Is that you? Is Sparky Anderson in town? I got him good in Detroit a couple of years ago. He owes me. Am I on fucking *Candid Camera*?"

"You're not listening."

"Ed Jerusalem is an over-the-hill nobody who actually never was. He's a fucking mop-up man. Only an asshole would even say his name in the same breath as Eckersley's."

"I said he has the potential to be another Eckersley. I wanted to get your attention. He has more ability than one might think, and . . ." a pause for effect, "if I were to teach Jerusalem my fadeaway pitch I'm certain he could fulfill his potential."

THE
FADEAWAY

Murtagh tries to recall what he knows of Christy Mathewson. He pitched for John McGraw's New York Giants. He was intelligent, a gentleman in a ruffian's sport. He was a graduate of Princeton or one of those snotty eastern colleges. Probably something of a psychologist, too — he could even get along with John McGraw, one of the toughest, most tempestuous and profane figures in the history of the game. McGraw loved Mathewson, treated him like the son he never had.

Mathewson had three-hundred-and-some wins — what had he just said, 343? Half as many losses, a minuscule ERA, shutouts galore, including three consecutive in the 1905 World Series against the Cubs. His winning pitch was the fadeaway, a reverse curve that would be called a screwball today.

"And just how the hell would you teach Jerusalem your fadeaway?"

"I'd teach you, and you'd teach Jerusalem."

"I don't know anything about teaching pitchers, that's Griff Wilson's job."

"We mustn't involve anyone else."

"This is crazy," says Murtagh, and hangs up the phone.

He stares down the third-base line at the green-padded left-field fence and the door to the bullpen, then walks back through the tunnels to the stadium exit, cautious, starting at shadows and the devious night sounds of the empty stadium. Murtagh goes home to his sleeping wife and a night of troubled dreams.

*   *   *

The next evening Cleveland builds up a comfortable early
lead. Good, Murtagh thinks. He doesn't have to plan any
strategy, for his mind isn't on the game. In the fifth
inning, even though his starter is in no trouble, Murtagh
looks around to make certain his pitching coach or bench
coach aren't watching and leans casually against the wall of
the dugout, blocking everyone's view of the bullpen
phone. He sneaks the receiver off the hook with his right
hand and places the earpiece awkwardly against his left ear.

"You didn't follow my advice."

"Your advice was horse shit," Murtagh replies.

"Did you win?"

"The press would have eaten me alive if I'd brought
in Jerusalem and he'd gotten hammered. I brought in
the best man for the job."

"And he got hammered. Two innings from now," the
voice continued, "your starter will be in serious trouble.
Bring in Jerusalem to pitch to the left-handed batter.
He'll strike him out on four pitches."

"We'll see," says Murtagh, glancing suspiciously over
his shoulder to find his pitching coach Snail Wilson
right behind him, frowning.

"What's up?" asks Wilson as Murtagh hangs up.

Murtagh doesn't know what kind of lie to tell. He is
not used to lying.

"Not much," he says feebly.

"So what were you discussing?"

Fucking paranoid pitching coach, thinks Murtagh.
He makes a small insincere laugh. "Just bullshitting
with Ed."

"Ed's been in the locker room since the third inning;
laying on the training table swilling Maalox. His ulcer's
been giving him shit." Wilson moves closer. "So what's
going on? You want to tell me?"

"No."

"No?"

"I'm the fucking manager. I can talk to the bullpen
any time I want to."

"What's the matter with you, Tag? You act like your
wife just caught you with your pants down in some
broad's bedroom."

"Leave me fucking alone," Murtagh yells, stomping off
to the far end of the dugout, ignoring the raised eyebrows
of the bench players.

As promised, two innings later things begin to fall
apart.

Tag is pleased to hear Ed's muffled "Yeah," at the other
end of the phone.

"How's the stomach?"

"I'll live."

"Good. Get Jerusalem and Robinson up," he says.

"Jerusalem?"

"You got a fucking hearing problem?"

Ed sighs like a Jewish mother, and hangs up.

"Who's warming?" Snail Wilson asks.

"Robinson," Murtagh says. "And Jerusalem."

"What the fuck for?"

"Precaution."

Now it is Wilson's turn to stomp away.

With the bases loaded and one out, Murtagh calls for Jerusalem to face the left-handed pinch hitter. He takes the ball from his starter, as Ed Jerusalem's hulking form steps from the bullpen onto the left-field grass.

"What are you bringing that mutt in for? He can't even pitch batting practice."

"When I need your input I'll ask for it."

The starter slams his glove to the ground and dropkicks it all the way to the dugout. The fans cheer and boo.

"Listen," says Snail Wilson, when Murtagh gets back to the dugout, "I want it made clear that I was opposed to bringing Jerusalem into the game. I got a big family. I don't want to be unemployed in the middle of the season."

"Witnesses!" Murtagh shouts to the bench. "Our pitching coach wants you to know he is opposed to bringing Ed Jerusalem into the game. I take full responsibility."

Ed Jerusalem throws the first pitch in the dirt. He follows with a fastball for a called strike, then something that resembles a screwball that the hitter misses by several inches. He then throws a real screwball that looks as if it will be a foot inside then barely scrapes the outside corner for a called strike three.

The starter spits, dangerously close to Murtagh's shoes, and stalks off to shower.

THE
FADEAWAY

Murtagh calls for Robinson, and walks toward the mound. Jerusalem stares at him with large, stunned brown eyes.

Robinson and the wild-eyed Panamanian closer each give up a run but Cleveland wins anyway.

Again, Murtagh waits until the stadium is empty before making his way to the dugout.

He lifts the cool yellow receiver from its silver hook.

"Perhaps now you believe me?" asks the voice.

"I saw, but I didn't believe it," says Murtagh.

"He threw the fadeaway only twice. It took all my strength to guide him. Had the hitter been any good he could have hit the first one. But the second was perfect."

"Why can't you do that all the time?"

"It takes enormous energy to guide someone else's mind and body."

"So, what now?"

"I shall teach you how to throw the fadeaway and you'll teach Jerusalem."

"Why Jerusalem? He's over the hill — and dumb as a plank."

"He has the perfect arm for the fadeaway. He'll last five or six seasons. He'll save thirty games between now and October and win the pennant for you."

Murtagh feels the adrenalin rush. A pennant, the World Series.

"Do you have a baseball?" Christy Mathewson asks.

The dugout is totally empty, swept clean.

"I'll get one," Murtagh says. He leaves the receiver swinging like a pendulum, and makes his way back to the clubhouse. He finds a perfect, virgin baseball and carries it back to the dugout.

"Shouldn't I get my pitching coach involved?" he asks. "He's the one who knows about pitching."

"You'll do it," Mathewson says. "Things would become hopelessly complicated if others became involved. I took a long look before choosing you."

"Why me?"

"You're basically honest and you're not greedy. Winning will be enough for you. Now listen, here's what you do . . ." and Christy Mathewson gives Tag Murtagh instructions on how to grip the ball, on how to stand on the mound, on where the pitcher's front foot should land to make the fadeaway most effective.

It takes over an hour.

"If I looked into the bullpen right now," Murtagh asks, "what would I see?"

"You'd see an empty bullpen, eerily blue with moonlight. I think 'essence' might be the best word to describe me."

"Will you be . . . around . . . if I need advice later on?"

"I've given you everything you need. You merely have to apply what you've learned."

"Apply it to Ed Jerusalem."

"That's right."

"I'll do my best."

THE
FADEAWAY

"No one can ask for more," says Christy Mathewson. The line goes dead.

Tag Murtagh sits for a long time in the empty stadium, Mathewson's words roaring in his ears. A pennant, a World Series. Tomorrow morning he will take Ed Jerusalem out to some deserted ballfield. He'll teach him the grip, the arm motion, the landing position. He'll catch him himself.

Out of the corner of his eye, Murtagh notices that someone has just entered the field from the radar booth behind home plate. It is Griff Wilson and he is carrying a video camera.

"Tag, can you explain what you've been doing here the last couple of hours? I'm worried about you, man."

"No, I can't," says Murtagh. "Something really important is going down. It's gonna win us a pennant. Please, please trust me." Murtagh can feel the hysteria rising in his voice.

"I was listening to you, man, you were carrying on a conversation with yourself. That ain't normal."

"Give me three days. I'll prove I'm not crazy."

"You're gonna make Ed Jerusalem your closer?"

"Trust me, please," Murtagh begs. "Three days. Three lousy days."

The pitching coach just walks slowly past Murtagh and into the tunnel leading to the locker room.

Griff Wilson had no choice. Murtagh knows he too would have gone to the owner if their roles had been reversed.

Within hours the owner announces that Griff "Snail" Wilson will replace Murtagh as field manager. Murtagh is being transferred laterally within the organization, his exact position and title to be determined and announced at a later date.

Griff Wilson's first act as manager of the Indians is to call up a young pitching phenom from Double-A, a twenty-one-year-old who has sixteen saves. To make room on the roster he places Ed Jerusalem on waivers for the purpose of giving him his unconditional release.

"Take a month off," the owner tells Murtagh. He is an amiable man, a self-made billionaire who manufactures women's undergarments and commercial fishing nets. "Make it two months. You've been working too hard. Go to Hawaii. Take a tour of Europe. No, I know. Take your old lady and go to Japan for a couple of months. Bring us back a Japanese shortstop. We'll call you Roving Pacific Rim International Scout. How does that sound?"

Murtagh shrugs.

Emptying his desk, he comes across the ball he used when he learned the fadeaway. He toys with it, turns it in his hands. He holds it the way Mathewson told him. He goes into a clumsy pitching motion, not releasing the ball. He will never teach Ed Jerusalem. He will probably never manage in the Bigs again.

THE
FADEAWAY

But maybe when he gets back from Japan there will be some Triple-A team in need of a manager. He will sign Ed Jerusalem to a minor-league contract. He will teach him the fadeaway . . .

What if I forget? Murtagh thinks.

He takes out a box of brand new baseballs, sets them, one by one, on the green felt desk pad like a herd of small exotic pets. He takes a purple stamp pad from the top desk drawer. Inking the fingers of his right hand carefully, he picks up a baseball with his left hand, and with great care grips it with his right exactly as Mathewson showed him. His fingerprints are burned into it like a brand.

Murtagh etches his fingerprints onto the baseballs, then rewraps each one in its square of tissue paper, closes up the box, puts elastic bands around it. He looks at his cartons of memorabilia and personal effects. Suddenly, he feels very tired. He will send for them later.

He places the box of baseballs under his arm and begins the long walk through the maze of dark tunnels to the blinding summer sun.

THE
DARKNESS
DEEP
INSIDE

If I'd never studied *Heart of Darkness*, I wouldn't have become involved with the Rev. Bascombe Jones. I think it's good that I became involved with the Rev. Bascombe Jones, but I seem to be the only one who thinks so.

Stark, the general manager, just called me a disruptive force. I am now inside the sleek, color-coordinated elevator full of tinkly, invisible music. Going down. "Gentle on My Mind." Nothing at the moment is gentle on my mind.

I take a deep breath. I am in control of my life. I cannot help how Stark, or the rest of management, or my fellow players feel about me. I am in control of my life because toward the end of last season, I dedicated my life to Christ. I was born again. I placed my life, and the lives of those I loved, in His hands. For better or worse. For better. For better.

A year ago, if Stark had called me into his office the way he did this afternoon, if he had said to me the things he said, I would have reached across his desk, grabbed a handful of his shirt and tie, lifted the little weasel out of his chair, and threatened to toss him through the tinted glass of his forty-third-floor office window. I'd have watched him turn pale, his chicken-sized heart palpitating with fear.

A year ago Stark's complaints against me would have been entirely different. Almost certainly — definitely — they would have been valid. I was never hauled on the carpet for anything I didn't do, until this season. Until *after* I changed my life.

Perhaps I slid out of the baseline to take out the short-stop as he tried to turn the pivot on a double play. Back then my slide was a rolling football block. I'd often leave a quivering mass of Dominican infielder in the general area of second base, semi-conscious, clutching a damaged knee or elbow or shoulder, as the ball rolled delicately into center field while runners ahead of me scored, and the runner behind rumbled past on his way to third. What I did was legal — infielders know their lives are on the line when it comes to turning the pivot. Still, because of my outright aggressiveness, I had a reputation as a dirty player.

If the umpire called me for sliding out of the baseline, I'd have a tantrum, scream and kick dirt, maybe ease off before the umpire tossed me, maybe carry on until I was ejected from the game. Twice last season I'd had to take on a second baseman who'd felt obligated to defend the honor of the grunt I'd just disabled. Both times we got tossed, and I ended up facing suspension from the Commissioner and getting lectured by Stark on sportsmanship.

Off the field, take no prisoners was my motto. There were more bar fights than I can remember. Some bleary-eyed computer salesman or hot-shot handball player who wanted to test his mettle against a real athlete would badmouth me — or my team, or our city, or the girl I was with, or some girl he just thought I was with — to get a reaction. I never disappointed. I'd be all over the guy like acid rain, usually with a solid left to the jaw that saved him several tooth extractions later in life.

Or, "Let's step outside," the would-be hero-whipper would slur, his sixth martini doing the talking.

"Can't right now," I'd say, smiling broadly, "because the guy behind you is a plainclothes cop."

When the guy turned to look I'd bury my fist in his belly, so deep my knuckles would feel his backbone. I loved their look of total surprise as they collapsed.

There was a great shot in the Los Angeles Times of four cops failing to bring me down. One was riding piggyback on me, another had his baton out looking for a place to land a blow. I drew a seven-game suspension for that escapade.

What the photograph didn't show was that about fifteen seconds later one of the cops drew his gun, pressed it against my heart and said, "You got five seconds to chill out or die."

I behaved for the rest of the road trip. Even at my wildest I knew what I was doing. When that cop stuck the gun in my chest I behaved like a lamb all the way to the station and until the team lawyer posted bail at 5:00 A.M.

My marriage and my possible divorce were a couple of the many reasons I got called into Stark's office this afternoon. Apparently, Jackie's lawyers are giving the club a bad time. Among the perks I've got in my contract are stock options. I don't think management wants any ex-wives as stockholders. And I don't want an ex-wife. I love Jackie. We've been married ever since Double-A ball in North Carolina. But ever since I stopped being irresponsible Jackie can't stand being around me.

Jacqueline Villaincourt. I fell in love with her name before I met her. She was a cousin of the catcher on our Double-A team. He flashed her picture in the locker room.

"I'm invited to Sunday dinner after the game tomorrow," he said. "She designs these fancy color ads you see in magazines."

"Take me with you," I said. "I think I'm in love."

"Get out of here, Griswold. I wouldn't let a relative of mine date an orangutan like you." He was only half kidding.

"What if it was a boy relative?"

"Not even then."

After the game we played poker. I fed him vodka and orange juice, let him win a little for a while. I was playing piss in the ocean, red deuces and one-eyed jacks wild, for cookies before I started school. Since the cookies might be the only food I was gonna see that day, I learned the intricacies of the game quickly.

"The way I figure, you owe me about two months' salary," I said to the catcher at the end of the evening.

He muttered a string of slurred obscenities.

"After the game tomorrow, take me with you to dinner at your gorgeous cousin's, and we're square."

"She's got a live-in boyfriend," said the catcher. "You're wasting your time."

"Maybe," I said.

"Just keep your fucking hands off her," said the catcher.

I smiled, not making any promises I didn't intend to keep.

Jacqueline Villaincourt was as beautiful as her name, curly black hair, deep brown eyes, a sweet Louisiana drawl, and a feistiness I found irresistible. Jackie was the kind of girl who thought she was never gonna take crap from any guy. I was a guy who dished out crap.

Jackie's live-in was a stockbroker barely as tall as she was, with a handshake like a cold pancake. I stared him into the sofa when we were introduced and ignored him for the rest of the evening.

After dinner I cornered her in the kitchen.

"You're the brightest and most beautiful woman I've ever met," I said. "I'm gonna steal you away from that accountant."

"Nobody steals me if I don't want to be stolen," Jackie said, licking her lips with a pointy pink tongue.

I decided she was the type who liked to be shocked. She was leaning against the kitchen counter. I had a hand on either side of her, clutching chrome and Arborite.

"You've got a pretty tongue," I said.

Then I stated what I guessed that tongue was good at.

She didn't even blush.

"You'll never know," she said, but the look in her eyes told me otherwise.

"Tell me I'm wrong," I said.

She almost smiled.

"You know, I've read all about you and your spoiled brat ways. I've even watched you play a couple of times. I think you're an asshole."

"I bet you like . . ." I said, naming a couple of passionate acts, smiling, making full eye contact.

She drew back her right hand to slap me. I had to be quick, but I caught her wrist, stopped her hand about an inch from my cheek.

"Tell me I'm wrong," I said again.

That was the first time Jackie surprised me. I'd spent the evening watching her face and figure. I hadn't noticed she was left-handed. I saw stars when her fist caught me alongside the head.

"That smarts. I've taken weaker shots from full-grown ballplayers."

"I was number two on the women's tennis team at Tulane."

"Let's go for a walk," I said. I still had hold of her right hand.

She surprised me again by leading me toward the back door.

That was six years ago, and Jackie's been surprising me ever since.

We were married eight weeks later. It was one of those hokey baseball weddings, right before the Saturday-night game. Some dreary little minister used about ten baseball metaphors for marriage, while the public address system threw his words back at him. We exchanged vows at home plate, then walked through a canopy of bats held by my teammates, while the ballpark organist assassinated the Recessional.

About the fifth inning, a guy yelled from behind third base as I was heading in from the outfield, "Hey Griswold! What kennel did you buy your bride from?"

I went straight into the stands after him and hammered him about fifteen times before my teammates pulled me off him. I think the team had to pay him $4,000 for his trouble and the cost of having his cheekbone set. But, considering the circumstances, neither the team nor the league suspended me. I'm sure they also took into consideration that I was leading the league in home runs and RBIs, and was gonna have a 40/40 season — forty home runs and forty stolen bases.

When I signed with the pros out of college my agent shook down my major-league team for a million-dollar signing bonus.

"Just wail the hell out of the ball and keep your nose clean," my agent told me. "Five years from now you'll be earning $3 million a year on a long-term contract."

Well, the five years are almost up, and Justin Birdsong was right. I've wailed the hell out of the ball, though I haven't kept my nose clean until this season, when the general manager calls me a disruptive force.

The elevator music has switched to "Sweet Caroline."

"We've never liked you very much," Stark said a few minutes ago. "But in a business relationship, we don't have to like you very much. Fans like to come out to boo a loud-mouthed jerk, to see what asshole trick he's gonna pull next. But now you're playing bad baseball and you're not even colorful any more."

I wanted to leap out of my chair and go nose to nose with him, to scream, "I don't like you very much either!" But I remained calm. I turned the other cheek.

Then he listed all the ways I was letting the team down. My home-run production was way down, my RBI total was off nearly 50 percent. The same with stolen bases.

"I'm adjusting to my new lifestyle," I said, keeping my voice level. I cracked my knuckles, imagining the sound to be the vertebrae in Stark's neck snapping.

"Where you're really letting us down," said Stark, "is leadership. You've always been aggressive, an example to the other players. But," he said, pausing meaningfully, "this religious conversion, or whatever it is . . ."

"I can be a Christian and still be aggressive," I said.

"Then do it. What it looks like to us is you've traded your balls for a Bible."

"Mr. Stark," I said, "I thought you'd be happy that I was settling down. Remember how you yelled at me when I threw that bat into the stands two years ago? You threatened to send me to the minors last summer, the day after I broke the Toronto second baseman's ankle. You did the same when I spiked the Cincinnati first baseman at the All-Star Game."

"You were colorful," Stark said. "Colorful and controversial. Color and controversy bring fans out to the ballpark."

"I'm trying to play the game fairly," I replied reasonably. "I try to invoke the Golden Rule — would I want some player to slide into me with his spikes in my face?"

At university I was on an athletic scholarship. I took four physical education courses. One of them was called Baseball History. We watched old baseball films like *The Babe Ruth Story* and *Fear Strikes Out*. There were never any exams in the athletes' courses, just pass or fail, and if I attended half the classes I got a pass.

But there was one fly in the ointment. I had to take a first-year English literature course — and pass it — in order to graduate. It did in most of the guys on the team. I looked at it as a challenge.

"I'm not dumb," I said to my advisor. "I've just never had any reason to pay attention to academic stuff, but I want my degree. I don't like the idea of failing."

"We'll get you a tutor," my advisor said.

"As long as it's a girl," I said.

Her name was Cheryl. About every third girl on campus was named Cheryl that year, and probably three hundred of them were pretty in the same interchangeable way.

"I've never really studied English," she said. "It just sort of comes naturally."

"The way I play baseball," I said. "If you teach me enough to pass this course, I'll teach you all about bats and balls."

She wasn't even a challenge.

She was barely average in bed but she was a good English tutor. I had to read *Heart of Darkness* by Joseph Conrad, which is this story about a Belgian trader who goes to the Congo and ends up going native and going mad.

The book was too long and too difficult, so Cheryl read it out loud to me, fifteen pages a day. She'd sit across the room and read, and wouldn't let me get out of my chair, even to get a Coke, until she'd finished that day's reading. Then she'd jump on me and we'd have sex until we were worn out. Afterward, in the damp and tangled sheets, she'd discuss what we'd read of *Heart of Darkness*.

One day she wouldn't let me even take off her bra until I memorized Joseph Conrad's real name. He was a Pole, and his real name was about a yard long with more K's and Y's than should be legal in America. That name stayed with me until the final exam, then floated away forever, along with Cheryl's last name, if I ever knew it. But I remember a lot about *Heart of Darkness*. Too much.

"It's like a western," I said. "A guy travels to the frontier and gets bushed. My old man used to tell stories his father told him about old cowboys and homesteaders in Nebraska who either took themselves a squaw and started dressing and thinking Indian or went mad from being alone and just got stranger and stranger until they ran off into the wilderness to die, or maybe killed themselves. *Heart of Darkness* is the same story, only set in Africa."

"Maybe, but that's irrelevant," said Cheryl. "What does Kurtz, the trader, say when he's dying?"

"'The horror, the horror.' Big deal!"

"It is. It's what the whole book is about. What is the horror he's referring to?"

"Africa?"

"No. He's looked inside himself. And what he sees is nothing but blackness. He's empty at the core. Instead of standing up for his principles he took the easy way, let himself go native, became a barbarian, did things no civilized man would do."

I passed my exam. Received my degree. Signed my major-league contract. But I remembered more than I wanted to about that Belgian trader, Kurtz.

I first saw the Rev. Bascombe Jones on television. A depressing Sunday in Minneapolis. It was about seven in the morning and I was twisting the dial, hoping for a Chuck Norris movie or some World Wrestling Federation bouts. I'd been out until 4:00 A.M. with a couple of girls I'd met at a nightclub. They'd taken me back to their apartment, deciding, I guess, that there was enough of me to go around. They were tireless. They said the same about me.

I'd been thinking as I spun the dial on the TV. When I was a kid being bounced from one person who didn't want me to another, I thought having more money than I could spend would be the answer. Here I was, a major sports star who could have almost anything I wanted. And I was downright unhappy.

Suddenly, there was the Rev. Bascombe Jones, a tall, lean fellow with slicked-back hair and a serious demeanor, wearing a white suit with a red rose in the lapel, a white silk ascot, and shoes like Fred Astaire danced in with Ginger Rogers.

"Brothers and sisters. There is a darkness deep inside us all, a sludge of the soul, the 3:00 A.M. of our lives . . ."

He was looking right at me when he said it. And suddenly I was so tired of doing what I was doing, I wanted to surrender. There had to be something more.

I felt as if the Rev. Bascombe Jones was speaking to me personally. That he could see me from the television, that he cared about me and was about to reach his long arm out from the TV and clasp my shoulder.

He was making the call for his audience to come forward and be saved, put their lives in His hands. They could cleanse that darkness deep inside.

Rev. Bascombe Jones was reading my mind. He knew the questions that had been plaguing me. He knew I was having troublesome thoughts.

"I feel empty at the core," I said into the telephone in that hotel room in Minneapolis. The voice that answered the Redemption Line, the 800 number, was young and resonant and sincere. "I'm really successful at what I do," I went on. "I'm married to a beautiful woman. I earn well over a million dollars a year. But I'm worried and unhappy, and I don't know why. I've got that darkness deep inside me, just like the Reverend was talking about, and I want him to help me get rid of it."

I didn't even know some of those things until I said them into that telephone.

"The Rev. Bascombe Jones will take your call personally," the young voice said. "Don't y'all go 'way now. You may have to hold for a couple of minutes."

*　　*　　*

"Don't ever divorce your first wife," was the one piece of advice my old man gave me. "Get married young and move on right quick. Then every girl you meet you can say, 'I'd love to marry you, honey, but I already got a wife.' Ha!"

My old man was a long-distance trucker, mainly hauling cattle out of the San Antonio stockyards. His wife was somewhere in Arkansas. He'd be on the road for a week or ten days at a time. He never drank a drop on the road, not even a beer with supper at the end of the day's drive. But when he came home he wanted to raise some hell, and usually did. He trashed our trailer house more than once.

"Looks worse than the time the tornado dropped in on us," Mama said once. We were out in the yard picking up a lamp and some sofa cushions my old man had pitched through a window, after he'd bashed it out with a coffee table.

I guess Mama figured she'd be worse off on her own, and that she could put up with a violent man for two or three days a month in return for a roof and a bed and three meals a day for her and me and my kid sister.

Once, before I started school, Mama was sick for a long time, must have been nearly a year. My sister was just a baby and the old man farmed her out to a cousin in Oklahoma. I rode in the truck cab and slept when I was sleepy and ate when I was hungry, and I learned to play piss in the ocean, first with truckers and then with some of the old man's relatives in Odessa, where he dropped me off for a good six months.

There were no women in the household, just a lot of cousins and uncles named Billy Ray and Travis and Butch. We used to play poker for Oreos and Twinkies, and if I didn't win I didn't eat. I promised myself that when I grew up I was gonna be some kind of famous and take general revenge on my old man and his unwashed relatives.

When I got my signing bonus I bought Mama a house of her own in Florida. Mama is only in her early forties, but she looks older; she's thin and seems like she's spent all her life looking over her shoulder, listening for the rumble of my old man's truck pulling into the gravel parking lot of the trailer park. My kid sister is in college now, studying to be a criminologist. I'm picking up the tab for her, too.

What Mama did after I bought her the house really disappointed me. She let the old man move in with her. I thought she'd get shed of him as soon as she was financially independent. She did set up a few ground rules, like he had to divorce that wife and marry her. Which he did. I'm told he sits in a sports bar in Boca Raton, Florida, and brags on me. He was especially proud when I used to get my ass continually in trouble. I suppose he's disgusted with me now, too.

"You don't know what it's like being lonely," was all Mama said, when I asked how come she let the old man tag along and freeload off her.

*   *   *

The Thursday after I spoke with the Rev. Bascombe
Jones, my team had a day off. Instead of spending
the day with Jackie, I chartered a plane and flew to
Tennessee.

"I am a great admirer of your skills as a baseball player," were the first words the Rev. Bascombe Jones spoke
to me in person.

I explained, as best I could, about being drug up in a
trailer park downwind of the San Antonio stockyards. I
told him that even though I was successful professionally
and financially beyond my wildest hopes, I felt uneasy,
afraid, hollow.

"There must be something else to life," I said.

"Indeed there is," said the Rev. Bascombe Jones.
"Indeed there is, my son."

Surrender was the key word.

"The Lord is there to bear your crosses for you," the
Rev. Bascombe Jones said. "All you have to do is ask."

He explained how I would have to change my life. I
could give up stimulants; I never was much of a drinker,
I remembered what my old man did when he was
drunk. I'd have a difficult time keeping my mouth clean.
A sportswriter once wrote that I had a seven-word
vocabulary, six of them beginning with f.

The most difficult change to make had to do with my
marriage. I did enjoy road trips. I had a dozen girls in
every city, all listed in a little black book crammed with

names and addresses and ratings on how good each girl was at sex.

When we were first married I said to Jackie, "The way to get along with and hold onto a ballplayer is never to ask what goes on on the road."

And Jackie, who has never ceased to surprise me, said, "That only works if it applies both ways."

"What do you mean?" I said, though I knew perfectly well what she meant.

"If you plan to play around on the road, then I am allowed to have intimate male friends here at home," gives the jist of what she said. Jackie's language was considerably earthier.

"Either way is fine with me," she went on, "just so long as we both know how things stand. If you claim we're going to be true to each other, I will cut your heart out if I ever catch you fucking around behind my back. You may be able to hit a baseball a ton, but you're not smart enough to go behind my back and not get caught."

So Jackie and I made this agreement, which I didn't confide to the Rev. Bascombe Jones. Whatever I did on the road, and whatever Jackie did while I was on the road, was our own business. But now that I was straightening up my life, that agreement was going to have to go.

"I don't think my wife is gonna take too kindly to our association," I told the Rev. Bascombe Jones.

"God has decreed that a man is the head of his household. Woman is there to serve. That is God's will." The Rev. Bascombe Jones handed me a book with a handsome white dust jacket with blue lettering. "The title is self-explanatory, son. Let your wife read it. It will explain her role in marriage, which is one of subservience. You may have to assert yourself a little at first, but she'll come around." I glanced through the book, which was mainly about women going against God's will by bobbing their hair, talking sassy to their menfolks, and desecrating their bodies by wearing men's clothing.

When I got home from my personal interview with the Rev. Bascombe Jones, I started up a big fire in one of the fireplaces, even though it was too warm for a fire.

"I want you to see this, Jackie," I started. "This is my black book," I said, flipping the pages so she could see it was full of names and addresses. "This has the names and numbers of all the women I know, or have known while I've been on the road. I opened the glass doors of the fireplace and tossed the book into the flames.

"I am gonna be faithful to you for the rest of my life," I said. "And that is a solemn promise you can take to the bank."

Then I told Jackie about my visiting the Rev. Bascombe Jones, about our conversation and my conversion, about how my life was gonna be a whole lot different, and how her life was gonna have to change some too.

I gave her the blue-and-white-covered book.

THE DARKNESS
DEEP INSIDE

"Are you fucking crazy?" Jackie said. "Those greaseball TV evangelists are all frauds. You've said so yourself a thousand times. They're against everything in life that's fun, or might be fun. They especially hate women, because they're afraid of them. What you do is your own business. If you want to get involved with a charlatan like Jones, it's your own funeral. But if you think I'm taking on any of this phony religious shit, you can think again."

She glanced at the book and tossed it in the fire.

I tried to explain how I felt. I especially tried to explain the facts as the Rev. Bascombe Jones outlined them. A man was the head of his household. Women serve. Men provide.

Jackie laughed.

"You better fish what's left of your address book out of the fire. You're gonna sorely miss it when you come to your senses. As for me, I have close male friends I am not about to give up while you are on the road."

I told her it was time to quit her job with the advertising agency even though she'd just been promoted. I said it was time for us to start a family, that I wanted a big family. I told her it was time for her to let her hair grow out full and natural, and that from now on we were going to run a pure Christian household, no stimulants, no alcohol, no coffee, no tea, no chocolate.

"You're going to have to stop smoking," I told Jackie.

I never have smoked, though I did chew a little tobacco on the playing field. I quit that the first time

the Rev. Bascombe Jones and I prayed together and I
turned my life over to the Lord. Nothing but sugar-free
gum and diet soda from then on.

"I can remember when you thought my smoking was
about the sexiest thing in the world," Jackie said, looking
at me the way she did when she was about to jump my
bones. "You tellin' me sex can't be any fun any more
either? That I'm gonna have to throw away all my sexy
lingerie, and the toys we got beside the bed, and that
leather garter belt . . ." And Jackie reached for me in that
way she has that makes me feel like my blood's turned to
hot sauce.

"You're gonna get over this in a month or two,"
Jackie said, after we'd done about everything a man and
woman can do to each other. "You hang around that
reverend for any length of time, you maybe won't feel
empty any more. Because you'll be full of shit, from the
top of your head to the tips of your toes." Jackie
laughed her sweet laugh, which reminded me of a
meadowlark's song.

"You let Jackie fix what's wrong with you," she
cooed. "You buy yourself one of them Italian sports
cars, help you forget your troubles. Next road trip to
New York you find yourself twin groupies like you
always fantasized. Then you come home and tell me all
about it, and I'll pretend to be both of them, and won't
we have us a time?"

THE DARKNESS
DEEP INSIDE

*   *   *

"It's called backsliding," the Rev. Bascombe Jones explained when I called his private line way deep in the night. "The flesh is weak," he said, "but the soul is stronger." We prayed together for over an hour.

"We're going to trade you," was Stark's final insult this afternoon, "if we can find a club willing to take over a fat contract on a slumping player who's a disruptive force on the ballclub."

Now, I've known players who became real idiots about being Christians. They handed out religious tracts in the clubhouse, and couldn't talk about anything but Jesus, and proselytized the other players until they got their lights punched out a couple of times. But I've never done that.

I let it be known that I was now a Christian, but I never talked religion to the other players. When something came up that I didn't want to do, like drink beer or chew or curse, all I said was, "I don't do that any more." I didn't even explain, though I sure wanted to.

When we came home from the next road trip I burned all of Jackie's sexy underwear, and all our sex toys and sexy books and videos, along with a whole bunch of Jackie's indecent clothes and tight blue jeans. It was a mistake for me to do that. It was a mistake to call the clothes indecent in front of Jackie. I considered that I was asserting myself as a husband was required to do, showing leadership.

That was the first time she left me. There have been two or three times since. This last one is most serious. She has retained a lawyer who represents lady movie stars in divorce actions.

I've appeared on the Rev. Bascombe Jones's Inspirational Television Ministry, shown on 141 markets in 34 states, I don't know how many times. Whenever we play an afternoon game, right after it's over I fly to Tennessee. Sometimes we do the show at midnight, but it always looks like Sunday morning. The choir is there in their blue and gold robes, the girl singer in her white dress with her upswept blond hair. The assistant pastors in their black jackets, white pants, red carnations in their lapels. The Rev. Bascombe Jones, all in white, tells my story better than I can tell it. Then I come forward and shake hands with everybody, give the girl singer and Mrs. Bascombe Jones a kiss on the cheek, and commence my witnessing. I talk mainly about turning the other cheek.

"I no longer play out of hate but out of love," I tell the camera.

I explain how what I've done hasn't been easy for me. How I have been pressured by management to continue my unfair play, how some of my teammates threaten me because they are threatened by me, how some of them play sick jokes on me. I tell the story of how the manager said to me one day after I went 0/5, striking out three times, "You've lost your spirit."

"No, sir," I said. "I've found the Spirit."

THE DARKNESS
DEEP INSIDE

The audience always likes that one. After the taping they all come around to hug me and shake my hand and tell me to have courage and trust in the Lord.

"You should have taken that son of a bitch out!" the manager roared last week, after I was forced at second base as the first half of a double play.

"I play by the rules," I replied matter-of-factly. "If the infielder had been at the base I'd have gone for him. But he was outside the line by the time I got there."

"You're a pussy, Griswold," the manager began, but I tuned him out. I mentally turned the other cheek.

I met Jackie for lunch a couple of days ago. I tried again to explain that her lifestyle is leading her straight to hell.

"This is gonna cost you, you son of a bitch," Jackie said, holding a copy of the legal papers I have been served.

"The church has a counseling program, the Rev. Bascombe Jones himself is involved. I know he'd counsel us personally if I asked. I can charter a plane . . ."

"And what would he counsel me?" asks Jackie.

She's so beautiful my heart seems to lurch sideways in my chest.

"He'd give me a copy of that fucking book, *Bobbed Hair and Whatever*. Let me tell you something, Greg Griswold. You think life is hard now? You think management is tough on you? You think the players are on your case? You think the umpires give you a bad time? Well, you just wait. Try throwing a rolling block at me and my lawyer. Slide into us with your spikes up."

"I don't do that any more," I say reasonably.

"You don't do anything any more, do you?"

"Don't you love me even a little bit, Jackie?"

"I love that wild-eyed barbarian who talked dirty to me in the kitchen of my condo six summers ago. I knew you were a bad risk as a husband, but your audacity, your unpredictability turned me on. And those are the qualities that still turn me on. You've traded it all for some phony eternal life. Well, I hope you enjoy your eternal life, because you're gonna suffer like hell in this one."

I go from Stark's office to see my lawyer. While I'm waiting, I think about a couple of girls at the church; sweet, shy girls with fervent eyes, dressed in modest pastels, waist-length hair not even decorated with barrettes. One of those girls would be grateful for a healthy, wealthy, successful husband. She'd be happy to stay home and look after her family. She wouldn't object to the word *obey* in her wedding vows.

I'm riding down in another elevator to a rinky-tink version of "Red River Valley." My lawyer had nothing but depressing news. As soon as I get home I'll call Rev. Jones's prayer line.

My personal darkness is down but not out. According to the Rev. Bascombe Jones, it will never be out, only under control. I wake in the night to the sound of its breathing. It is there, chittering like something out of a horror movie, palpable, that darkness deep inside. I reach for the phone.

EGGS

It is February. The past months have been nothing but Februarys. I'm only thirty-one and my arm feels fine, but my fastball is gone. All last season I survived, if anyone could call it that, on cunning, an only partially successful screwball, and my former reputation as the best pitcher in baseball. My ERA was 5.97, I only appeared in thirty-six games, my record was 1-6. I averaged over twenty wins in each of the previous nine years, but when my long-term contract expired the Angels showed no interest in renewing.

"You've had a great career," management told me, not even in person. "You're financially secure. Enjoy your retirement, get on with your life."

"I'll work all winter developing a knuckleball, maybe try a split-finger fastball, perfect the screwball," I told my agent. "Get me a contract, with anybody." What I wanted to say was "I'm only somebody when I'm on the mound. I'm only somebody when the ball smashes into the catcher's mitt and the batter twists into a corkscrew. I need one more season before I can adjust to retirement." But that would have sounded pathetic.

"Look, Webb," said my agent, "through the wonders of instant replay every team in organized baseball has footage of you being bombed every time you stepped on the mound last season, and you know your trouble started in the middle of the previous season."

"I know, but I'm getting stronger," I lied. There is something wrong with me. I feel weak, drained. Even though doctors can't find anything, I keep thinking cancer, leukemia.

"If we could claim you'd been injured it would be different, teams will hang in with you forever in hopes that you'll rehabilitate," my agent went on. "But there's no physical cause for your decline. One of the weaker teams may give you a Triple-A contract, gambling that you improve. Do you really want that? You don't need the money."

Then last week the expansion Florida Marlins, a team desperate for any kind of pitching, came through: an invitation to spring training as a non-roster player, but still a chance to make the team, to prove I'm not through. Every has-been pitcher who can still lob a base-ball will be in that camp. I will have to swing a bat, face a live pitcher for the first time since I was in the Pioneer League, eleven years ago.

EGGS

I've pitched regularly all winter, run ten miles a day (I have my own indoor track), exercised, lifted weights. I've even taken batting practice, for I have always had a pitching machine in the basement of the multi-million-dollar house on the cold, isolated Alberta prairie where I spend the off-season.

But it is February outside and February in my heart. My pitching has not improved over the winter, if anything my fastball is weaker, my knuckleball too wild and too slow. I'm only thirty-one. But I'm tired. Twenty-four hours a day I feel an ecstatic lethargy, as if I've just had sex.

The idea of swinging a bat again bothers me more than I care to admit. I wake in the night with a lurch, sticky and unrested. I am flying backward out of the batter's box, only as I fall the ball is following me, curving in on my face. I wait in terror for the sickening sound of baseball on bone. Then the ball is suddenly full of brilliant geometric designs, like the easter eggs that Maika and my mother-in-law Halya decorate at the kitchen table. I can smell the paint and the vinegar odor that always accompanies their enterprise. My wife, my mother-in-law, foreign, patterned eggs.

I glare at the fluorescent smirk of the clock on the night table. February, 3:00 A.M. I stare at the shape of my sleeping wife, Maika, wondering how she can rest in such tranquility, while beside her, troubled, I dodge chin music from a terroristic pitcher.

"Retire," seems to be the only word in Maika's vocabulary these days. "Koufax retired young," she reminds me repeatedly. "Don't be a Steve Carlton, begging to try out in Japan, a pathetic shadow of yourself. We have no financial worries, you'll be elected to the Hall of Fame the first year you're eligible."

"Quit to do what?" I wail. "I'm a baseball player. I don't know anything else."

"You don't need to know anything else," Maika points out. "We have investments: this house, what? two, three million in the bank? Don't be like those old boxing champions, ex-champions, their brains all puffy, still fighting years after they should have retired with dignity."

A completely reasonable argument. But wrong.

"If I retire, I won't continue to live here," I say to Maika, not knowing I was going to say that. "I think living here in Alberta has contributed to what's wrong with me."

"But there's nothing wrong with you," Maika says with a terrible logic that I don't want to hear. "The team paid for the best specialists in the world to look at you — your arm, your back. Some athletes wear out before others. You just have to accept that."

But I do not accept that. I cannot explain why I will not retire. I cannot explain to Maika or her mother Halya, who lives with us, though it is almost as if we live with her.

If I did attempt to explain to Maika, I would say something like, "I know I'm as good a pitcher as I've always been. There's nothing physically wrong with me, there's nothing mentally wrong with me either. I think you and your mother are sapping my strength, conspiring to force me to retire, distancing me from, isolating me from baseball." I also suspect they may be trying to kill me, may have put some curse on me. But I could never say that out loud. It would sound too crazy.

I can hear the fuss even a hint of my accusation would cause. I can feel Maika and Halya fluttering around me, trying to put me at ease, exchanging worried glances, letting me know as politely as possible that they think me mildly demented. What can I say? I have no proof, just an eerie feeling that they are doing something out of the ordinary. Something wicked.

I met Maika Osadchuk the first year I won twenty games in the Bigs. We were married as soon as the season was over. She was a flight attendant working the Los Angeles–Honolulu run. When I first saw her she was wearing a bluebird-colored uniform that contrasted with her brown eyes and coppery skin; her hair was dark but with a twinge of fire to it. I thought she might be part Indian, or perhaps from Peru or Bolivia. She turned out to be more exotic, at least to a boy who had lived all his life protected by the green Allegheny Mountains. Her family had emigrated to Canada from the Ukraine when her grandmother was a girl. Her great grandfather had been a Cossack. She had a tinted photo of him mounted on a rearing black horse, wearing a sky-blue tunic and brandishing a curved, silver sword.

The first time I ever saw a decorated egg was at the tiny apartment Maika shared with another flight attendant she seldom saw.

"What is that?" I asked, pointing at the only decoration on the narrow, varnished mantel above the fake fireplace.

"You've never seen a painted egg?"

"It's egg-shaped, but is it really an egg?"

"Of course. I painted it myself. My mother taught me, and my grandmother taught her. Painting eggs is the Ukrainian national pastime, like baseball here in the States."

I picked it up, was astonished by its lightness. In spite of what Maika said, I had expected that it would be made of stone or crockery.

I turned the brilliant sphere in my hand, rolled its multicolored geometric designs down to the tips of my long fingers, transferred it to my pitching hand.

"The egg is always blown dry. You poke a tiny hole in each end and blow out the insides."

"Like a vampire in reverse."

"Sort of."

"What do the designs mean?"

"They tell stories, some of them. They go way back, pre-Christian. They're a bit like cave drawings: history, myth, tall tales. Every home has to have one. 'A decorated egg assures a good harvest,' my grandmother used to say, 'and wards off evil.' And then she'd shake her finger under my nose, 'and assures you many babies.'"

"It looks to me as if the harvest has been good," I said, staring at Maika and smiling, "and I don't see any evil to ward off. I'll pass on the babies though, at least until we get to know each other better." I replaced the egg on the white candy dish.

After the honeymoon, Maika insisted on taking me home to Canada to meet her family. Her mother lived in a town called Vegreville, in rural Alberta, nearly three hundred miles north of the Montana border. As a rookie I had played in the Pioneer League, traveling to dusty towns in Montana and southern Alberta, so I wasn't totally unprepared for the dryness of the air, the high sky and open spaces. But I had never spent a winter anywhere really cold and decided my imagination was not large enough to imagine forty below.

"You're seeing Alberta at its best. The fall is the most beautiful time of year. Indian summer — the crops being harvested, everything golden."

Everything was indeed golden, I had to admit, the sky a distant baby blue where hawks circled, thin and black as coat hangers. The flatness was awe-inspiring, an occasional red or green combine lumbering like a dinosaur, grain elevators visible in almost every direction, buoys on a golden ocean.

It was not an elevator that greeted us as the highway narrowed to pass through Vegreville, but a massive painted egg.

It stood on end, some twenty feet tall, many feet in diameter, an intricate geometric design in a rainbow of colors.

Once, during the summer, Maika had demonstrated the art of egg painting. She had produced a box of dyes and watercolors and over a long weekend had transformed a large white egg into a kaleidoscopic wonder of color and design.

"Does it tell a story?" I asked.

"Boy meets girl, boy gets girl."

We built our home on the outskirts of Vegreville. The town council considered printing postcards of THE WEBB WATERMAN HOUSE to send out with their thousands of postcards of the giant painted egg, but when Halya heard of the idea she persuaded the mayor that it would be as insensitive as the American news media. The plan was scrapped. But on warm Sunday afternoons cars arrive from as far away as Edmonton, some sixty miles distant, slowing on the gravel secondary road to behold the glass and aluminum marvel that is the family home of Webb Waterman, professional baseball pitcher.

Halya already owned the quarter section of land on the outskirts of Vegreville, or Wag-re-will, as she and the older settlers of Ukrainian descent pronounce it. My mother-in-law and her friends wear their accents proudly, like Germans wear leather pants.

I've never been sure how I came to build a permanent home in Alberta, a cold, dry, windy place tolerable only because Maika's roots are here. I remember on our first visit, walking the barren land as Maika and Halya discussed where the house would sit, where the access roads would be. I was very much in love. Maika's body could keep even the Alberta cold at a distance.

I had no idea how long a project our house would turn into. Halya was quick to adjust to having a wealthy son-in-law.

The house, built at the apex of my career, cost close to $2 million. It is over seven thousand square feet. Separated from the pool by Plexiglas panels is my pitcher's mound, an exact duplicate of the one in Anaheim Stadium, with a padded strike zone sixty feet, six inches away, and a portable silhouette of a six-foot-tall batter to give my practice authenticity. (I stand six foot seven and have a long, sorrowful face, brick-colored hair, and pale skin covered in penny-sized freckles.)

At first, except for the murderous climate, I wasn't too dissatisfied with my winter home. In my secure mansion on the edge of a small town where baseball was something Americans played, where the guys who played hockey and curling (a game resembling shuffleboard on ice) were local heroes, I was comfortable.

My mother-in-law, though she appeared to be no more than fifty, liked to pretend she was old, even infirm. Halya was a thin, sharp-featured woman, who must have been a rather beautiful brown-eyed blond. When I first met her she seldom left her house, a small frame building painted a searing bachelor's-button blue and stuffed to bursting with sofas, box chairs, and dark, wooden furniture.

Halya spent her days sitting at her highly polished dining-room table, usually wearing a garish kimono, her hair protected by a flowered babushka, coloring eggs and all the while talking on the telephone to her friends, usually in Ukrainian.

According to Maika, Halya would herd her friends into the living room to show off her egg collection and her pictures of me. She had a large portrait of me in uniform, our wedding picture, plus a collection of framed photographs of me — covers from *Sports Illustrated*, *The Sporting News*.

"I'm not sure I like her doing that," I said to Maika, when she continued the practice after we moved into the new home, sometimes even when I was in the house. "There's something unnatural about it. That collection of photographs is like a shrine."

"She's just proud of you," said Maika lightly.

Maika's father was never mentioned. There were no photos. "He left when I was very young," was all Maika had said.

"I can't stand it here any more," I said to Maika for about the twentieth time this winter. I was mentally packing for spring training, though I couldn't leave for at least two weeks. I was not going to spend another winter staring out across the snow-crusted prairie in the depressing purple light of afternoon.

"We've been over this before," said Maika, her voice pleasant and reasonable. "Who would ever buy this house?"

"We can afford to live anywhere we want to. This tundra . . . it's weakened me."

Maika smiled at what she obviously considered my foolishness. "The kids love it here, they have their friends. Besides, Mother could never leave Alberta."

The wind-whipped snow was sculpted in ice-cream shapes along the edge of the runway where my twin-engined plane with the golden baseball insignia on the tail sat, cold and forlorn.

"Halya was here before we came, she can stay after we're gone. She'll just have a better house to live in," I said. "Maybe Florida, if I catch on with the Marlins. Florida is warm, green, a person's blood can circulate there. I think that's what's wrong with me, I'm like someone who has fallen through the ice on one of these lakes, my body has slowed to a standstill. If I stay any longer I'll suffer brain damage."

I longed to challenge Maika's loyalty to her mother, to point out that her mother would have no part in any decision to move. If Halya chose to follow us that was fine. If she didn't, even better. But after all, who would want to continue to live in this bleak, cold, dry climate?

As I became more determined to leave Alberta for good, Maika, always a sweet and ardent lover, became more passionate, more artful.

All this winter, Maika and Halya have decorated eggs. There are eggs everywhere, in groups on china plates in the dining room, glowing like candies in soft baskets on the sideboards, on the TV, on the children's dressers. Even my daughters work with their mother and grandmother at the kitchen table, their brows furrowed, their stubby fingers colored by dyes.

Once I came upon Maika bent at the table; she had her lips against the end of a large, brown egg. The contents were dribbling into a glass.

"Eeech!" I said, immediately queasy.

"Omelettes for supper," said Maika, but all I could see for hours was the sickly liquid trickling down the side of the glass.

Sometimes events puzzle me. I wake in the deepest hours of the night to find Maika gone from our bed. I continue to sleep, but fitfully. Eventually I feel the gentle vibrations of her feet as she crosses the carpeted room. As if aware of my restlessness, Maika frees the covers at the foot of the bed and burrows upwards. Her breath on my legs brings me erect. I hear her familiar cooing sounds, always associated with lovemaking, before I feel her mouth and tongue on me, hot, slicing away the lethargy of sleep.

Eventually I pull her up to me and we make love for a long time, after which I fall into a deep, exhausted sleep.

Could this passionate lovemaking be part of Maika's strategy to keep me from moving to a warmer climate? I can imagine Maika and Halya discussing what they can do to thwart my plan. A number of times recently, they have looked conspiratorial, speaking Ukrainian.

I imagine Halya's leathery voice saying, "A satisfied man does not want to go hunting. Feed him well and do your homework every night."

But, I am going to do things my way. I will play one more year, more if I recover my strength. I will move my family to a warm climate. Maika can choose the location, but I will force *some* choice on her.

For the second time I wake with a lurch, hurling myself backward, away from a ball destined for my face, but this time the ball was a decorated egg streaking toward me.

Maika is not beside me. Must be nearly dawn. I am about to drift into sleep again when something touches my foot.

"What?"

"Shhh!" comes Maika's familiar whisper. Her warm hand reaches in under the blankets, caressing my leg.

I lie back, anticipating that Maika will follow her hand.

I hear a scuttling sound at the end of the bed, a scuffing on the carpet, the vibrations of someone moving across the floor toward the door. Has one of the children wandered in after a bad dream? I know I am not imagining it. I wait for the subtle change in air patterns that will tell me the door has opened and closed in silence. The breath of air comes, and with it an odor that cuts like ammonia.

I jerk wide awake.

The odor that frightens me is of things wizened, of decay, the vinegary smell of dyes, Halya.

I grab Maika's arm and pull her roughly to the top of the bed. Then I flood the huge room with light.

"What's wrong with you?" asks Maika, annoyed. "It's the middle of the night." She is tucking a dark breast back inside her blue satin nightgown.

"Halya's been in this room," I shout. "What's going on?"

"Go back to sleep," says Maika.

I grab her wrist, stopping her from turning off the lamp.

"You've had a bad dream."

"It wasn't a dream. She was here. I can smell her."

Maika smiles her sexiest smile. "Come close," she croons. "Let me cuddle you."

I grab the bed clothes and sweep them from the bed. My long, naked body looks pale and vulnerable against the midnight-blue bottom sheet. I stare suspiciously at myself, at Maika, at the bed.

"Let me get the covers," says Maika. As she leans across the bed she slips down the top of her nightgown exposing her dark-nippled breasts.

As my eyes get used to the bright light, I feel a little foolish. I am about to say so, about to apologize for being rough with her. Maika's hand is once again reaching for the light when I run my hand down between my legs, rub curiously, discover a sickly wetness, withdraw my hand.

I howl in anguish for it appears my fingers are covered with blood. I leap from the bed and bolt to the washroom, wrench a towel from the rack and stuff it between my legs. I've heard that, when first mutilated, victims feel no pain. In the operating-room brightness of the washroom, I examine my hand. My fingers are not covered with blood but colors. My fingers stink of paint and vinegar.

"Come back to bed," comes Maika's voice from outside the door.

I yank the door open. "Get away from me." I stand above her, fist raised. When she sees my wildness she flees.

I ease the soft, white towel from between my legs. I examine myself carefully, studying the colors smeared on the towel. Turning on the shower full blast, I make it as hot as I dare before stepping in. I soap myself extravagantly, watching in fascinated revulsion as the water, tinged with blue, ochre, scarlet, green, runs down my legs, and swirls around to the drain.

Barefoot, I move stealthily through the dark, carpeted rooms. A yellowish light glows like a long scar at the foot of Halya's door. I think I can hear organ music, the muffled voices of my wife and mother-in-law, anxious, plotting.

As I lope through the rooms the eggs are lying in wait for me. I can almost hear their insidious clicking as they tremble to life.

"You can't do anything to me," I call through the gray light of the living room to the row of eggs standing on the mantel, like monks in colorful robes. Going from room to room I gather what must be a hundred eggs; I have to make two trips. When I am finished the pitching machine is full, and the auxiliary basket overflows with the intricately decorated eggs.

The long February of my life is over. Come dawn I will warm up my plane and fly off to spring training, where the sun will cook my pale arms and forehead, where I will regain my strength, where my arm will snap on every pitch like a flag in a brisk breeze. I don socks and cleats, turn up the lights until they are bright as sunlight. I dig in at the plate, press the switch to activate the pitching machine, hold my bat high, and wait.

HOW
MANNY
EMBARQUADERO
OVERCAME
AND BEGAN
HIS CLIMB
TO THE
MAJOR
LEAGUES

For me, the baseball season ended on a Tuesday night last August at the exact moment that Manny Embarquadero killed the general manager's dog.

In a season scheduled to end August 31, Manny arrived July 15, supposedly the organization's hottest prospect, an import from some tropical island where the gross national product is revolution, and the per capita income $77 a year. A place where, it is rumored, because of heredity and environment, or a diet heavy in papaya juice, young men move with the agility of panthers and can throw a baseball from Denver to Santa Fe on only one hop.

According to what I had read in USA Today, there were only two political factions in Courteguay — the government and the insurgents — depending on which one was currently in power. One of the current insurgents was a scout for our organization, reportedly receiving payment in hand grenades and flame-throwers. He spotted Manny Embarquadero in an isolated mountain village (on Manny's island, a mountain is anything more than fifteen feet above sea level) playing shortstop barefoot, fielding a pseudo-baseball supposedly made from a bull's testicle stuffed with papaya seeds.

Even a semi-competent player would have been an improvement over our shortstop, who was batting .211, and was always late covering second base on double-play balls.

"The organization's sending us a phenom," Dave "The Deer" Dearly told us a few days before Manny's arrival. Dearly was a competent manager, pleasant and laid-back with his players. A former all-star second baseman with the Orioles, he knew a lot about baseball and was able to impart that knowledge. But on the field during a game, he was something else.

"Been swallowing Ty Cobb Meanness Pills," was how Mo Chadwick, our center-fielder, described him. Dearly was developing a reputation as an umpire-baiting bastard, who flew off the handle at a called third strike, screamed like a rock singer, kicked dirt on umpires, punted his cap, and heaved water coolers onto the field with little or no provocation.

"Got to have a gimmick," he said out of the side of his mouth one night on the road, as he strutted back to the dugout after arguing a play where a dimwitted pinch runner had been out by thirty feet trying to steal third with two out. Dearly had screamed like a banshee, backed the umpire half way to the left-field foul pole, and closed out the protest by punting his cap into the third row behind our dugout. The fans love to boo him.

Before Manny Embarquadero arrived, my guess was that Dave Dearly would be the only one on the squad to make the Bigs.

I planned on quitting organized baseball at the end of this season. My fastball was too slow and didn't have enough action; my curve was good when it found the strike zone, which wasn't often enough. I was being relegated to middle relief way down here in A ball — not a positive situation. I could probably make it as far as Triple-A and be a career minor leaguer, but I wasn't that in love with minor-league baseball. I've got one semester to a degree in social work, and I'd enrolled for the fall.

I'm a Canadian, from Tecumseh, Ontario, not far from Windsor, which is connected by bridge to Detroit.

I agreed with Dearly that unless you were Roger Clemens or Ken Griffey, Jr., you needed a gimmick. As it turned out, Manny Embarquadero had a gimmick. If the ball club hadn't been so cheap that we had to bunk two-to-a-room on the road, I never would have found out what it was.

Manny Embarquadero looked like all the rest of those tropical paradise ballplayers, black as a polished bowling ball, head covered in a mass of wet black curls, thin as if he'd only eaten one meal a day all his life, thoroughbred legs, long fingers, buttermilk eyes.

The day Manny arrived, the general manager, Chuck Manion, made a rare appearance in the clubhouse to introduce the hot new prospect.

"Want you boys to take good care of Manny here. Make him feel welcome."

Manny was standing, head bowed, dressed in ghetto-Goodwill-store style: black dress shoes, cheap black slacks and a purple pimp-shirt with most of the glitter worn off.

"Manny not only doesn't speak English," Chuck Manion announced, "he doesn't speak anything. He's mute. But not deaf. He knows no English or Spanish, but follows general instructions in basic sign language.

"The amazing thing is he's hardly played baseball at all. He wandered out of the mountains, was able to communicate to our scout that he was seventeen years old and had never played competitive baseball. He truly is a natural. I've seen video tapes. The way he plays on one month's experience, he'll be in the Bigs after spring training next year."

Chuck Manion was a jerk, about forty, a blond, red-faced guy who looked as if he had just stepped out of a barber's chair, even at eleven o'clock at night. Any time he came to the clubhouse, he wore a four-hundred-dollar monogrammed jogging suit and smelled of fifty-dollar-an-ounce aftershave. His family owned a brewery — and our team. Chuck Manion played at being general manager just for fun.

"I bet he thought he'd get laid a lot, was why he wanted a baseball team as a toy," said my friend Mo Chadwick, one night when Manion, playing the benevolent, slumming employer, accompanied a bunch of players to a bar after a game. He seemed extremely disappointed that there weren't dozens of women in various stages of undress and sexual frustration crawling all over.

"Sucker thought he'd buy one round of drinks and catch the overflow," said Mo.

He was right. Manion hung around just long enough for one drink and a few pointed questions about Baseball Sadies. As soon as he discovered that minor-league ballplayers didn't have to beat off sex-crazed groupies, he vanished into the night.

"Going down to the airport strip to cruise for hookers in his big BMW," said Mo. Again I had to agree.

After we all shook hands with Manny Embarquadero and patted him on the shoulder and welcomed him to the club, Manion made an announcement.

"We're gonna make Crease here" — he placed a hand on my shoulder — "Manny's roommate both at home and on the road. Crease reads all the time so he won't mind that Manny isn't much of a conversationalist." Manion laughed at his own joke.

I did read some. In fact, I'd been involved in a real brouhaha with my coaches because I read in the bullpen until my dubious expertise was needed on the mound. The coaches insisted that reading would ruin my control. I read anyway. I was threatened with unconditional release. I learned to hide my book more carefully.

Management rented housekeeping rooms within walking distance of the ballpark. My last roommate had gone on a home-run-hitting binge and had been promoted directly to Triple-A Calgary.

My nickname, Crease, had come about because ever since Little League I'd creased the bill of my cap right down the middle until it's ridged like a roof above my face. I always imagined I could draw a straight line from the V in the bill of my cap to the catcher's mitt.

"This guy is too good to be true," Mo Chadwick said to me after we'd watched Manny Embarquadero work out. "Something's not right. If he's only played baseball for one month, how come he knows when to back up third base, and how come he knows which way to cheat when the pitcher's going to throw off-speed?"

"Ours not to reason why," I said. "He's certainly a rough diamond."

If Manny Embarquadero hadn't talked in his sleep, I never would have found out what a rough diamond he really was.

On our first night together, I woke up in humid blackness on a sagging bed to the sound of loud whispering. The team had reserved the whole second floor of a very old hotel, so at first I assumed the sounds were in the hallway. But as I became wider awake, I realized the whispering was coming from the next bed.

Apparently no one was certain what language, if any, Manny Embarquadero understood.

"Our scout says he may understand one of the pidgin dialects from Courteguay," Chuck Manion had said the day he introduced Manny. The mountains Manny had wandered out of bordered on Haiti, so there was some speculation that Manny might understand French. Needless to say, we didn't have any French-speaking players on the team.

I raised the tattered blind a few inches to let a little street light into the room, just enough to determine that Manny was alone in bed. What I was hearing was indeed coming from his mouth, but it wasn't Spanish, or French, or even some mysterious Courteguayan dialect. It was ghetto American, inner-city street talk pure and simple.

He mumbled a lot, but also spoke several understandable phrases, as well as the words "Mothah," and "Dude," and "Dee-troit." At one point, he said clearly, "Go ahead girl, it ain't gonna bite you."

At breakfast in the hotel coffee shop, Manny, using basic hand signals and facial expressions, let me know he wanted the same breakfast I was having: eggs, toast, hash browns, large orange juice, large milk, large coffee.

"I think we should have a talk," I said to Manny as soon as we got back to the room after breakfast.

Manny stared at me, his face calm, his eyes defiant.

"You talk in your sleep," I said. "Don't worry, I'm not going to tell anyone, at least not yet. But I think you'd better clue me in on what's going down."

Manny stared a long time, his black-bullet pupils boring right into me, as though he was considering doing me some irreparable physical damage.

"If I was back home, Mon, that stare would have shrivelled your brain to the size of a pea," Manny said in a sing-songy Caribbean dialect.

"Your home, from what I heard, is in Detroit," I said, "somewhere with a close-up view of the Renaissance Center. So don't give me this island peasant shit. When I look closely I can tell you're no more seventeen than I am. You're older than me, and I just turned twenty-three. I don't know why you're running this scam, and I don't particularly care. But if we're gonna room together you're gonna have to play it straight with me."

"Fuck! Why couldn't I draw a roomie who's a heavy sleeper? I really thought I'd trained myself to stop talking in my sleep."

The accent was pure inner-city Detroit, flying past me like debris in the wind.

"So what's the scam? Why a mute, hot-shot child prodigy of a shortstop from the hills of Courteguay?"

"I just want to play baseball."

"That's no explanation."

"Yes, it is. I played high-school ball. I didn't get any invites to play for a college. I went to every tryout camp in the country for three years. Never got a tumble. 'You're too slow, you don't hit for power. Your arm is strong but you don't have enough range.' If you ain't the most talented then you got to play the angles. I seen that all the shortstops were coming from Courteguay, and they're black, and I'm black, so I figured if I went over there and kept my mouth shut and pretended to be an inexperienced kid from the outback, I'd get me a chance to play."

His words went by like bullets, but I've captured the gist of what he said.

"Shows a hell of a lot of desire," I said.

"I even tried the Mexican Leagues, but I couldn't catch on."

"But in a month or so, when you don't improve fast enough, this team is going to send you packing. Back to Courteguay."

"I'm gettin' better every day, man. I'm gonna make it. People perform according to expectations. Everyone figures I'll play my way into the Bigs next spring, and I'm not gonna disappoint them."

"There's a little matter of talent."

"I have more than you can imagine."

"Lots of luck."

The next night, when Manny played his first game, the play-by-play people mentioned that Manny was mute but not deaf. By the eighth inning, there were a dozen people behind our dugout shouting to Manny in every language from Portuguese to Indonesian. Manny shrugged and smiled, displaying a faceful of large, white teeth.

He was a one-hundred-percent improvement on our previous shortstop. I could see what the scouts, believing him to be seventeen and inexperienced, had seen in him. He had an arm that wouldn't quit. He could go deep in the hole to spear a ball on the edge of the outfield grass, straighten effortlessly, brace his back foot on the grass, and fire a rocket to first in time to get the runner. He covered only as much ground as was necessary, never seeming to extend himself, but covering whatever ground was necessary in order to reach the ball.

Of course, his name wasn't Manny Embarquadero.

"I am one anonymous dude. Jimmy, with two m's, if you must know, Williams with two l's. Hell, there must be two thousand guys in Dee-troit, Michigan, with the same name. And all us young black guys look alike, right?

"I had a Gramma, probably my Greatgramma, but she died. I think I was her granddaughter's kid. But that girl went off to North Carolina when I was just a baby and nobody ever heard from her. Once, Gramma and I lived for three years in an abandoned building. We collected cardboard boxes and made the walls about two feet thick. It gets fucking cold in Dee-troit, Michigan. Gramma always saw to it that I went to school."

Two nights later, there was a scout from the Big Show in the stands. Everyone pressed a little, some pressed a lot, and everybody except Manny looked bad at one time or another. Manny was unbelievable. One ball was hit sharply to his right and deep in the hole, a single if there ever was one. The left-fielder had already run in about five steps, expecting to field the grounder, when he saw that Manny had not only fielded the ball, but was directly behind it when he scooped it up and threw the runner out by a step. What he did was humanly impossible.

"How did you do that?" I asked, as he flopped on the bench beside me after the inning. Manny just smiled and pounded his right fist into his left palm.

Later, back at the hotel, I said, "There was something fishy about that play you made in the sixth inning."

"What fishy?"

"You moved about three long strides to your right and managed to get directly behind a ball that was hit like lightning. No major-league shortstop could have gotten to that ball. You're not a magician, are you?"

"I'm not anything but a shortstop, man." But he looked at me for a long time, and there was a shrewdness in his stare.

What I could not understand was that no one else had noticed that one second he was starting a move to his right to snag a sure base hit, and an instant later he was behind the ball, playing it like a routine grounder. When I carefully broached the subject, no one showed any interest. He had not even been overwhelmed by congratulations when he came in from the field.

I admired his audacity. It troubled me that on one of my many visits to Detroit to see the Tigers, the Pistons, or the Red Wings, I may have passed Manny/Jimmy on the street, in one of those groups of shouting, pushing, swivel-jointed young men who congregated outside the Detroit sports facilities.

The trouble between Chuck Manion and Manny Embarquadero began on a hot Saturday afternoon, before a twinight doubleheader. Chuck Manion, wearing a sweatsuit worth more than I was getting paid every month, showed up to work out with the team. He was accompanied by his dog, a nasty spotted terrier of some kind, with mean, watery eyes and a red ass. Manion sometimes left the dog in the clubhouse during a game, where it invariably relieved itself on the floor.

"After losing in extra innings, it's a fucking joy to come back to a clubhouse that smells of dog shit," The Deer said one evening.

"Tell him where to stuff his ugly, fucking dog," one of the players suggested. We all applauded.

"Wouldn't I love to," said Dearly. "Unfortunately, Manion's family actually puts money into this club. An owner like that can do no wrong."

On that humid Saturday afternoon, Manion brought the dog out onto the playing field. Dearly spat contemptuously as he hit out fungoes, but said nothing.

Manny and I were tossing the ball on the sidelines, when

Manion pointed to Manny and said to me, "Tell Chico to take Conan here for a couple of turns around the outfield."

"His name is Manny," I said. "And he can understand simple sign language. Tell him yourself."

"You're the one who's retiring end of the season, aren't you?" Manion asked me in a snarky voice.

"Right."

"And a goddamned good thing."

He walked over to Manny, put the leash in his hand and pointed to the outfield, indicating two circles around it.

I wondered what Manny Embarquadero would do. I knew what Jimmy Williams would do. But which one was Manion dealing with?

It didn't take long to find out.

Manny Embarquadero let the leash drop to the grass, and gave Manion the finger, staring at him with as much contempt as I had ever seen pass from one person to another.

Manion snarled at Manny and turned away to hunt down Dave Dearly. At the same moment, Conan nipped at Manny's ankle.

Manny's reaction was so immediate I didn't see it. But I heard the yelp, and saw the dog fly about fifteen feet into left field, his leash trailing after him.

Manion found Dave Dearly, and demanded that Manny be fired, traded, deported, or arrested.

"Goddamnit, Chuck," Dearly responded, "I got enough trouble babysitting and handholding twenty-five players,

most of them rookies, without having you and your goddamned mutt riling things up."

The mutt, apparently undamaged, was relieving himself on the left-field grass, baring his pearly fangs at any
ballplayer who got too close.

Manion continued to froth at the mouth, threatening
Dearly with unemployment if he didn't comply.

At that moment, Dearly must have remembered his
reputation as an umpire-baiter. His face turned stop-sign
red as he breathed his fury onto Chuck Manion, backing
him step by step from third base toward the outfield,
scuffing dirt on Manion's custom jogging outfit. Manion
had only anger on his side.

"Take your ugly fucking dog and get the fuck off my
baseball field," Dearly roared, turning away from Manion as suddenly as he had confronted him. Dearly punted his cap six rows into the empty stands, where it landed right side up, sitting like a white gull on a green
grandstand seat.

Manion retrieved the dog's leash and headed for the
dugout, still raging and finger-pointing.

"From now on walk your own fucking dog on your
own fucking lawn," were Dearly's parting words as
Manion's back retreated down the tunnel to the dressing
room.

The players applauded.

"Way to go, Skip."

*　　*　　*

"You better watch out," I said to Manny, over a late supper at a Jack-in-the-Box. "Manion's gonna get your ass one way or another."

"Fuck Manion and his ball club," said Manny Embarquadero. "And fuck his dog, too."

Manion didn't show his face on the field all the next week, but he could be seen in the owner's box, a glass wall separating him from the press table, pacing, smoking, often taking or making telephone calls.

Manny continued his extraordinary play.

"Did you see what I did there in the second inning?" Manny asked in our apartment after the game.

"I did."

"I can't figure out how I did it. If anybody but you sees . . . what would they do, bar me from the game?"

In the second inning, Manny Embarquadero had gone up the ladder for a line drive. The ball was far over his head, but I saw a long, licorice-colored arm extend maybe four feet farther than it should have. No one else, it seemed, saw the supernatural extension of the arm. They apparently saw only a very good play.

"Want to tell me how you do what you do?" I said.

Manny had made at least one impossible play in each of the last dozen games. At the plate it was less obvious, but probably magically inspired as well. He was batting over .400.

"Must be because you know who I really am that you

can see what I do," said Manny. "Besides, no one would believe you; I'm just a poor, mute, black, immigrant ballplayer."

"I've no intention of spreading your secret around. I'm going to be through with baseball for good in a few weeks."

"If you want a professional career, I might be able to arrange it. It would involve a trip to Courteguay. And I don't know, you being white and all."

"Not interested."

"There's a factory down there. They sing and chant over your body, wrap it in palm fronds, feed you hibiscus petals and lots of other things. After a week or so, you emerge from the factory with an, iron arm and the speed of a bullet and the ability to be in more than one place at a time.

"It's just like a magic trick, only the whole ballplayer is quicker than the eye. They send a couple of guys up to the Bigs each year. I just lucked out. I really thought I'd stand a chance of getting a professional contract if I came from a backwater like Courteguay. The reason I got into the factory, got the treatment, was I got caught stealing food that supposedly belonged to this guerrilla leader, Dr. Noir. Looks like Idi Amin, only not so friendly . . ."

"What do you have to do in return?"

"You don't want to know," said Manny.

"Probably not. You're kidding me, right? There's no factory in Courteguay that turns out iron-armed infielders."

"Think whatever you want, man. This Dr. Noir was from Haiti: voodoo, dancing naked all night, cutting out people's spleens and eating them raw. At the moment Dr. Noir leads the insurgents in Courteguay, but some day soon he'll be president again."

"You're right," I said. "I don't want to know."

A week later, after a short road trip, Dave Dearly was fired. We were in first place by a game, thanks mainly to Manny Embarquadero's fielding and hitting.

The grapevine reported that Chuck Manion had been unable to convince the parent club to get rid of Manny. Dave Dearly was another matter. Since Manion and his family put large amounts of their own money into the stadium and the team, the top dogs decided that if keeping him happy meant jettisoning a minor-league manager, so be it.

The third-base coach, a young guy named Wylie Keene, managed the club the next night.

"It was because The Deer went to bat for your Courteguayan friend over there," Keene told me. "Chuck Manion wanted Manny given the bum's rush out of baseball. But The Deer stood up to him.

"He told the parent club that he wouldn't have his players treated that way, and life was too short to work for an asshole like Manion. But, we all know money is the bottom line, so The Deer is gone. He thinks the organization will find another place for him."

"What do you think?"

"I don't know. He's a good man. He'll catch on somewhere, but not likely in this organization."

When we got home I passed all that information to Manny.

"Manion is a son-of-a-bitch," Manny said. "I'd love to get him to Courteguay for a few minutes. I'd like to leave him alone in a room with Dr. Noir. Hey, he's got a degree in chiropractics from a school in Davenport, Iowa. Dr. Lucius Noir. I saw his diploma. According to rumors, he deals personally with political prisoners. Just dislocates joints until they confess to whatever he wants them to confess to. Wouldn't I love to hear Manion scream."

"Look, you're gonna be out of this town in just a couple weeks. You'll never have to see or hear Manion again."

"But there is something I have to do. Come on," he said, heading for the door.

"It's after midnight."

"Right."

We walked the darkened streets for over half an hour. Manion's house overlooked the eighteenth tee of a private golf course. It loomed like a mountain in the darkness.

"Listen," I said. "I'm not going to let you do something you'll be sorry for, or get arrested for . . ."

"Don't worry, I'm not going to touch him. The only way you can hurt rich people is by taking things away from them."

We crawled through a hedge and were creeping across Manion's patio when Conan came sniffing around the corner of the house. He stopped abruptly and stood stiff-legged, fangs bared, a growl deep in his throat.

"Pretty doggie," said Manny Embarquadero, holding a hand out toward the hairless, red-assed mutt. They stood like that for some time, until the dog decided to relax.

Manny struck like a cobra. The dog was dead before it could utter a sound.

"I should have killed Manion. But I've got places to go."

"Somebody's gonna find you out."

"How? Are you gonna tell? In Courteguay they'd barbecue that little fucker. Dogs are a delicacy."

"You're not from Courteguay."

Manny was going to get caught, there was no doubt in my mind. He was going to ruin a promising baseball career, which may or may not have been aided by the supernatural. Personally, I had my doubts about Manny's stories, but I admired his chutzpah, his fearlessness.

"Manny Embarquadero is pure magic. They'll never lay a hand on me," said Jimmy Williams.

"You forget," I said, "There isn't anyone named Manny Embarquadero."

"Oh, yes, there is," he said. "Oh, yes, there is."

As we crawled through the hedge, I let a branch take the creased cap off my head. A bus passed through town at 4:00 A.M., and I'd be on it.

SEARCHING
FOR
JANUARY

On December 31, 1972, Pittsburgh's all-star outfielder Roberto Clemente took off on a mercy flight taking clothing and medical supplies to Nicaraguan earthquake victims. Some time that night his plane went down in the ocean. His body was never recovered.

T he sand is white as salt but powdery as icing sugar, cool on my bare feet, although if I push my toes down a few inches, yesterday's heat lurks, waiting to surface with the sun.

It is 6:00 A.M. and I am alone on a tropical beach a mile down from our hotel. The calm ocean is a clear, heart-breaking blue. Fifty yards out a few tendrils of sweet, gray fog laze above the water; farther out the mist, water, and pale morning sky merge.

It appears slowly out of the mist, like something from an Arthurian legend, a large, inflatable life raft, the depressing khaki and olive-drab of military camouflage. A man kneeling in the front directs the raft with a paddle. He waves when he sees me, stands up and calls out in an urgent voice, but I can't make it out. As the raft drifts closer I can see that the lone occupant is tall and athletic-looking, dark-skinned, with a long jaw and flashing eyes.

"Clemente!" is the first word I hear clearly. "I am Clemente! The baseball player. My plane went down. Days ago! Everyone must think I am dead."

What he says registers slowly. Clemente! It has been fifteen years. Is this some local fisherman playing a cruel joke on a tourist?

"Yes," I call back, after pausing too long, scanning his features again. There is no question: it is Roberto Clemente. "I believe everyone does think you're dead."

"We crashed on New Year's Eve," he said. "I'm the only one who survived."

He steps lithely into the water, pulls the raft up on the beach, tosses the paddle back into the raft.

"Five days I've been out there," he says. "Give or take a day. I sliced up the other paddle with my pocket knife, made a spear. Caught three fish. Never thought I'd enjoy eating raw fish. But I was so hungry they tasted like they were cooked. By the way, where am I?"

I tell him.

He thinks a minute.

"It's possible. We crashed at night on the way to Managua. The plane was carrying three times the weight it should have, but the need was so great. Supplies for the earthquake victims.

"You look so surprised," he says after a pause. "Have they called off the air search already, given us up for dead?" When I remain silent he continues. "Which way is your hotel? I must call my wife, she'll be so worried."

"I am surprised. More than surprised. You are Roberto Clemente, the baseball player?"

"Of course."

"You were lost at sea?"

"Until now."

"There's something not quite right."

"Like what?" says Clemente.

"Like what year do you think this is?"

"When we took off it was 1972, but New Year's Eve. We crashed in the ocean. It must be January fifth or sixth, maybe even the seventh, 1973. I haven't been gone so long that I'd lose track of the year."

"What if I told you that it was March 1987?"

"I'd laugh. Look at me! I'd be an old man in 1987. I'd be . . ."

"Fifty-two. Fifty-three in August."

"How do you know that?"

"I know a little about baseball. I was a fan of yours."

He smiles in spite of himself.

"Thank you. But 1987? Ha! And I don't like the way you said *was*. *Was* a fan of mine." He touches spread fingers to his chest. "These are the clothes I wore the night we crashed. Do I look like I've been wearing them for fifteen years? Is this a fifteen-year growth of beard?" he asks, rubbing a hand across his stubbly chin. "A six-day beard would be my guess."

His eyes study me as if I were an umpire who just called an outside pitch strike three: my pale, tourist's skin, the slight stoop as if the weight of paradise is too much for me.

"Say, what are you doing out here alone at dawn?" Clemente says skeptically. "Are you escaped from somewhere?"

"No. But I think you may be. Believe me, it is 1987."

"Can't be. I can tell. I'm thirty-eight years old. I play baseball. See my World Series ring." He thrusts his hand toward me, the gold and diamonds glitter as the sun blushes above the horizon.

I dig frantically in my wallet. "Look!" I cry. "I'm from Seattle. Here's the 1987 Seattle Mariners schedule." I hold the pocket-sized schedule out for him to look at.

"Seattle doesn't have a team."

"They have a new franchise, since 1977. Toronto came in the same year. Read the schedule."

He studies it for a moment.

"It's crazy, man. I've only been gone a few days."

We sit down on the sand, and I show him everything in my wallet: my credit cards, an uncashed check, my driver's license, coins, and bills.

"Try to remember when your plane went down. Maybe there's a clue there."

We walk slowly in the direction of the hotel, but at the edge of the bay, where we would turn inland, Clemente stops. We retrace our steps.

"It was late in the night. The plane was old. It groaned and creaked like a haunted house. I was sitting back with the cargo — bales of clothes, medical supplies — when the pilot started yelling that we were losing altitude. We must have practically been in the water before he noticed. We hit the ocean a few seconds later, and I was buried under boxes and bales as the cargo shifted. A wooden box bounced off my head, and I was out for . . . a few seconds or a few minutes." He rubs the top of his head.

"See, I still got the lump. And I bled some, too." He bends toward me so I can see the small swelling, the residue of dried blood clinging around the roots of his sleek, black hair.

"When I woke up I was in front of the emergency door, the cargo had rolled over me and I was snug against the exit. The plane must have been more than half submerged. There was this frightening slurping, gurgling sound. Then I realized my clothes were wet. The raft was on the wall right next to the door. I pulled the door open and the ocean flooded in. I set out the raft, inflated it, and took the paddles and the big water canteen off the wall. I yelled for the others but I don't know if they were alive or if they heard me. There was a mountain of cargo between me and the front of the plane.

"I climbed into the raft, paddled a few yards, and when I looked back the plane was gone. I've been drifting for five or six days, and here I am."

"I don't know where you've been, but you went missing New Year's Eve 1972. They elected you to the Baseball

Hall of Fame in 1973, waived the five-year waiting period because you'd died a hero."

"Died?" Clemente begins a laugh, then thinks better of it. "What if I go back with you and call in?"

"You'll create one of the greatest sensations of all time."

"But my wife, my family. Will they all be fifteen years older?"

"I'm afraid so."

"My kids grown up?"

"Yes."

"Maybe my wife has remarried?"

"I don't know, but it's certainly a possibility."

"But, look at me, I'm thirty-eight years old, strong as a bull. The Pirates need me in the outfield."

"I know."

"My teammates?"

"All retired."

"No."

"If I remember right, Bruce Kison was the last to go, retired last year."

"Willie Stargell?"

"Retired in 1982. He's still in baseball but not playing."

"Then I suppose everyone that played at the same time, they're gone too? Marichal? Seaver? Bench? McCovey? Brock? McCarver? Carlton?"

"Carlton's won over three hundred games, but he doesn't know when to quit. He's a marginal player in the American League. So is Don Sutton, though he's also won three hundred. Jerry Reuss is still hanging on, maybe one or two others. Hank Aaron broke Babe Ruth's home-run record, then a guy from Japan named Sadaharu Oh broke Hank Aaron's record."

"And my Pirates?"

"Gone to hell in a handbasket. They won the World Series in '78, Willie Stargell's last hurrah. They've been doormats for several seasons, will be again this year. Attendance is down to nothing; there's talk of moving the franchise out of Pittsburgh."

"They need Roberto Clemente."

"Indeed they do."

"And Nicaragua? The earthquake?"

"The earth wills out," I said. "The will of the people to survive is so strong. . . . The earthquake is history now."

"And Puerto Rico? Is my home a state yet?"

"Not yet."

He looks longingly toward the path that leads to the hotel and town. We sit for a long time in that sand white as a bridal gown. He studies the artifacts of my life. Finally he speaks.

"If I walk up that path, and if the world is as you say — and I think I believe you — I will become a curiosity. The media will swarm over me unlike anything I've ever known. Religious fanatics will picnic on my blood. If I see one more person, I'll have no choice but to stay here."

"What are your alternatives?"

"I could try to pass as an ordinary citizen who just happens to look like Roberto Clemente did fifteen years ago. But if I become real to the world I may suddenly find myself white-haired and in rags, fifty-three years old."

"What about baseball?"

"I could never play again, I would give myself away. No one plays the game like Clemente."

"I remember watching you play. When you ran for a fly ball it was like you traveled three feet above the grass, your feet never touching. 'He has invisible pillows of angel hair attached to his feet,' my wife said one night, 'that's how he glides across the outfield.'"

"Perhaps you could go to the Mexican Leagues," I suggest. "Remember George Brunet, the pitcher? He's still pitching in the badlands and he's nearly fifty."

"I suffer from greed, my friend, from wanting to claim what is mine: my family, my home, my wealth. My choice is all or nothing."

"The nothing being?"

"To continue the search."

"But how?"

"I've searched a few days and already I've found 1987. Time has tricked me some way. Perhaps if I continue searching for January 1973, I'll find it."

"And if you don't?"

"Something closer then, a time I could accept, that would accept me."

"But what if this is all there is? What if you drift forever? What if you drift until you die?"

"I can't leap ahead in time. It's unnatural. I just can't."

"If you came back to baseball, Three Rivers Stadium would be full every night. You could make Pittsburgh a baseball city again. You'd have to put up with the media, the curious, the fanatics. But perhaps it's what you're destined to do."

"I am destined to be found, maybe even on this beach, but fifteen years in your past. I intend to be found. I'll keep searching for January."

He walked a few steps in the direction of the raft.

"Wait. I'll go and bring you supplies. I can be back in twenty minutes."

"No. I don't want to carry anything away from this time. I have five gallons of water, a bale of blankets to warm me at night, the ingenuity to catch food. Perhaps my footprints in the sand are already too much, who knows?"

He is wading in the clear water, already pushing the raft back into the ocean.

"If you find January . . . if the history I know is suddenly altered, I hope I went to see you play a few times. With you in the line-up the Pirates probably made it into the World Series in '74 and '75. They won their division those years, you know . . . you would have been the difference . . . ."

I watch him drift. Trapped. Or am I trapped, here in 1987, while he, through some malfunction of the universe, is borne into timelessness? What if I were to accompany him?

"Wait!" I call. "There's something . . ."

But Clemente has already drifted beyond hearing. I watch as he paddles, his back broad and strong. Just as the mist is about to engulf him, as ocean, fog, and sky merge, he waves his oar once, holding it like a baseball bat, thrusting it at the soft, white sky.

FEET
OF
CLAY

Mike Wheeler became known as Wheels not because of his last name but because of his legs. At his first high-school practice he took grounders in short left field, firing accurately to first, and tracked down pop-ups behind third base that no one but a professional could get to.

The coach, who didn't know any of the players, patted Mike Wheeler on the back as he came off the field and said, "For a short-assed kid you got a helluva set of wheels."

The nickname stuck through college, two years in minor-league baseball, and a twelve-year career as a shortstop with Kansas City and the Texas Rangers that didn't end until 1980.

Wheels Wheeler had no regrets when the Rangers cut him in the spring of what would have been his thirteenth season. He was financially stable, and had had a good solid career — he'd been a starting American

League All-Star three times, had a lifetime .291 batting average, had knocked in seventy-plus runs for eight consecutive years, and had five gold gloves.

On his retirement he vowed to keep in shape — when he came back as an Old Timer it would be at his playing weight, faster of foot and better coordinated than anyone his age. He had been revolted by the ex-players who showed up for Old Timers' Day looking as though they had been packing away five meals a day, washing them down with a dozen Buds, and not taking a lick of exercise. Even the ones still active as coaches were fifty pounds overweight and sporting jowls.

"I'd be embarrassed to death to show up for an Old Timers' Day looking like that," Wheels had said to a teammate as they watched the veterans pose for a group photo. "Did you ever see so much beef on the hoof?"

"They'd make a helluvan advertisement for a fat farm," his friend agreed. "But they've done their time. Let 'em enjoy themselves."

"But they were great athletes," argued Wheels. "How can they let themselves go like that?"

"Wait until you've been retired five years. They'll be calling you Training Wheels!" His friend laughed explosively.

"Man, I may become old, but I'm never gonna get fat, or lazy, or more inept than I have to," said Wheels. "I'm never gonna give up."

*   *   *

After Texas released him he considered playing in the Mexican Leagues just to keep active, but the desire wasn't there. In Mexico the pay was poor and the living conditions deplorable. Wheels had his agent make inquiries in Japan. A couple of Japanese teams even gave him a looksee, but the Japanese wanted their *gaijin* to be sluggers. There were plenty of slick-fielding Japanese shortstops.

Wheels Wheeler retired to his home state of Wyoming. He hadn't been a cowboy when he was growing up, though most of his friends had. His father had owned a drug store in a town of two thousand, not far from Casper. They lived on five acres of land four miles out of town and a thousand feet above it.

In his first full season with Kansas City, on a night when he'd had three hits and a stolen base against the Yankees, he'd been introduced to a girl in a New York nightclub and a few weeks later they'd become engaged. That winter he took her home to Wyoming.

She was tall and dark, a model for a New York agency. She looked a little like Anjelica Huston.

"How can you stand it here?" she asked, staring out the window down a long valley, at the snow-capped hills. "There's nothing here."

"There's everything here," he replied. He was stunned, inarticulate as he tried to explain his love of the open spaces, the high, glaring sky. "This is where I'm going to live after baseball. I'm going to build a house high on the sidehill overlooking the town."

"But what would you do? What would I do?"

"We'd enjoy our good fortune. We'd enjoy our friends."

"I could never live here," she said. "They shoot eagles in Wyoming. I read about it in the *Times*."

Wheels eventually married a girl from a ranch near Quitman, Texas. She said that the saddest part of living in Tulsa, where she was a computer programmer, was not having her own horse to ride.

Wheels and Willene (pronounced Wy-lene) spent a month in Miami. He convinced her to quit her job and come back to Wyoming with him. He bought her a horse, a prancing buckskin with pale eyes and a soft silvery nose. Willene walked with him to the spot where he planned to build their home. Her parents came in for the wedding. It was their first airplane flight.

The night before his wedding, Wheels Wheeler stared up at the hills above the town, could see the high-windowed house with the red tile roof that he planned to build, could see the white fences of the corrals, could see Willene's red hair blowing in the wind as she rode toward the summit on her proud buckskin.

Willene traveled with him to spring training.

A lot of the players were rough-and-ready types, willing to party all night and quietly nurse their hangovers in the locker room before games. Wheels minded his own business, but privately he marveled at their stupidity.

"I figure every beer you drink cuts ten games off your career," he told Willene. "Then there's hard liquor, and cigarettes, and drugs. These guys just don't think."

Early in his retirement Wheels stayed pretty close to home. Once in a while he'd throw out the first pitch at a high-school game, and the sportscaster on Casper TV would have him on to talk about each upcoming season. Once he flew to Denver to be guest speaker at a Society of American Baseball Researchers convention. These were men who lived and died for the statistics of the game. Many could tell you about every pitch of the 1904 season, but didn't know which team was currently leading the American League West.

Wheels entertained them with stories of how he and his teammates with the Royals once teased Andy Squilles, the All-Star first baseman, who was known for his ability to pack away food. Once they put a live piglet in his locker.

"Andy never cracked a smile, just nodded solemnly, put the piglet in his first baseman's glove and walked out of the locker room. An hour later he came back with a takeout carton full of crisp bacon and about twenty slices of toast. He sat in front of his locker and ate every bite.

Then he told his favorite Andy Squilles story, of how Andy had a girlfriend or two in every city in the American League, and he didn't think his wife knew about his off-field activities.

"She was a big-hearted gal who enjoyed a little fling herself when Andy was on the road, and she let the other wives know she had no illusions about what he did away from home.

"Well, in Chicago we found this girl with a really sexy voice. We paid her to phone Andy and make a date with him. Some of us claimed we knew this girl, that she was really something special — he had to wear his best suit and take candy and flowers and champagne. Andy went off for his date looking like a Republican senator or TV preacher. He was so laden with presents all he needed was a pointy paper hat to be going to a third-grade birthday party.

"The address this girl gave Andy was Room 702 in a downtown hotel. Several of us had got together and paid to fly in Andy's wife, Eudora, from Kansas City. And when he knocked on number 702 it was Eudora who opened the door.

"She said later Andy handled himself like a pro, or at least a semi-pro. Except for the first five seconds, when he looked like he'd been kicked in the gonads by a mule, he handled himself real well.

"'Surprise!' he finally said. And him and Eudora went on to have a wonderful evening.

"She kept asking him, 'How did you find out I was in town? I wasn't gonna call you for another hour.'

"But old Andy just smiled. 'There ain't nothin' us ballplayers don't know about our women.'

"Next morning we had that sexy-voiced girl phone Andy and ask where in the world had he been. She'd waited the whole evening for him, in room 207.

"Andy just couldn't believe his luck. He just sat by his locker and ran his hand through his rust-colored hair. Not one of us cracked up within his sight, ever. He'd been retired for several years before Eudora told him the truth."

The fifth year he was out of baseball Wheels became eligible for the Hall of Fame. He received eleven votes, which meant he'd never make it. The results came as no surprise: his statistics were good but not great.

It was the spring he turned forty-two, seven years after he was back in Wyoming, that the call came from his agent, Donnie Swift. Wheels had been asked to play in May on Old Timers' Day in Kansas City, and the sponsors were taking an option on him for eleven other Old Timers' games over the summer.

"I'm gonna show them that old Wheels Wheeler isn't that old," he said to Willene.

"You haven't played for seven years. Don't you go straining all your muscles and spraining all your bones."

"It's just a matter of timing and practice," said Wheels, "but I wish I had more than three weeks to get ready. At least I'm still at my playing weight, and I can walk five miles up the canyon without even breaking a sweat."

That evening he made a point of refusing dessert, even though the portion Willene gave him was half as large as hers and the children's. That evening, too, a group of businessmen asked Wheels if he'd be interested in running for the Wyoming state senate. But he was too excited about the Old Timers' games to do anything but put the men off indefinitely.

He had to drive all the way to Cheyenne to rent a pitching machine — hauled it home in the back of his King Cab, set it up so the broad back of the barn was a backstop. He spent two mornings leveling the corral, where he sketched out a baseball diamond.

He hired a high school boy from a neighboring ranch to hit him grounders, and he dragooned his son, Troy, who was fourteen and more interested in football than baseball, to play first base.

"I'm not going to embarrass myself," he told Troy. "When your Daddy takes the field in his Kansas City Royals uniform, he is going to be the best forty-two-year-old baseball player it's possible to be."

He practiced three hours every evening, until he wore out his hitter and fielder.

"Hit 'em harder!" he'd holler at the kid with the bat. "Try to get the ball by me. I used to field the hardest balls Dave Winfield could hit. I got to be able to do that again."

He rigged up a couple of makeshift floodlights so he could take batting practice after dark, figuring that if he could hit the best the machine could offer in this terrible light he should be able to knock the cover off any ball thrown by some forty-five-year-old pitcher.

At the banquet the night before the Old Timers' game he learned he was going to play shortstop to Kiko Alonzo's second base. He and Alonzo had been the starting double-play combination for the American League All-Star team one year. Alonzo was a chain-smoker who had added fifty pounds to his small frame. He wheezed amiably, "I am a rich man in my country. Also I have not had to pay for a drink or a meal since I retired."

It didn't look as if Kiko had turned down a single invitation since his retirement, but Wheels laughed jovially and patted Alonzo's paunch.

At the dinner, catered by Kentucky Fried Chicken, Wheels ate two pieces of white meat after carefully scraping off the crusty skin, two biscuits, and about a spoonful of gravy. The rest of his meal was coleslaw and a Diet Coke with lime.

Some of the Old Timers were, to put it kindly, three sheets to the wind. A huge first baseman, who had once led the National League in home runs, had a contest with a former MVP outfielder to see who could eat the most drumsticks. The winner was the ex-MVP who, Wheels figured, must weigh over three hundred pounds. He downed twenty-seven drumsticks, lining up the white bones in front of his plate in groups of five.

Before the game, the mandatory group photo was taken, flashbulbs popping, television personnel jockeying for position. Wheels looked from face to face — what was he doing in this group of large, aging men? He felt like a terrier at a convention of St. Bernards.

*　　*　　*

In the second inning, with a man on first, a fairly sharp ground ball was hit five steps to his left. Wheels backhanded the ball and flipped it perfectly to second for the double play. But Alonzo was still five steps from the bag and the runner not a third of the way down from first. The ball rolled into center field. Both runners were safe.

"E-6," somebody yelled.

Wheels kicked at the infield dirt until dust devils whirled around his ankles.

A moment later he made a diving stop of what was a sure single. This time he waited three beats while the third baseman got to the bag ahead of the runner, who was loping down to third as if walking his dog to the post office.

His first time at bat Wheels slammed the ball off the right-center-field wall. A stand-up double in the old days, but he eyed the center-fielder and decided to go for third, even though the other batters had settled for the nearest base. The throw in was slow and off the mark. Wheels slid into third in a cloud of dust, his foot expertly catching the corner of the bag.

"What the hell you trying to prove?" hissed the third baseman, as Wheels beat the dust from his uniform.

"I'm playing hard. It's the only way I know how."

"Well, ease up. Nobody wants to watch you show off."

His second time at bat he ripped the ball into the right-field corner. This time he didn't even pause going around second — triple all the way. Trouble was there was a lumbering outfielder on base in front of him. Wheels had to scramble back to second.

In the third inning he was replaced at shortstop by an ex-pitcher who wasn't going to get a chance to pitch. The ex-pitcher made two errors and the National League won 6-5.

"Wait 'til next time," Wheels muttered.

As soon as he got home Wheels began practicing for his next Old Timers' game, three weeks away. Saturday afternoon Wheels took batting practice for an hour, then drove his Jeep halfway up the canyon, got out and climbed the rest of the way, enjoying the effort, sweating slightly. Feeling strong and satisfied with life he stared down at the town in the valley, at his own red-roofed home on the sidehill.

Later, as he and Willene sat side by side watching the sunset, the phone rang. It was his agent.

"Donnie," Wheels said, "that Old Timers' Game was a blast. I gave them a show, I tell you. You should have seen me field . . ."

"Wheels," Donnie interrupted. "The Old Timers' Game is why I called. There's a problem."

"What problem? I have a contract for twelve appearances."

His agent cleared his throat a few times. "Wheels, after the game some of the guys complained that you made them all look bad."

"Complained!" Wheels practically screamed. "Who would complain — a bunch of slovenly oafs who don't have the willpower to push back from the table?"

"It's an Old Timers' Game, Wheels. Underline the word old. Nobody's expecting anything from you."

"Well, I'm expecting something from me. Sure I played hard. What do they want me to do, shuffle around like a slob, pretend I've had my feet on a footstool ever since I retired?"

"Look, Wheels — they just feel you don't fit in with the rest of the Old Timers. The sponsors have dropped your option."

"Can they do that?"

"I can read you the clauses in the contract if you like. I'm sorry, Wheels. There's nothing I can do."

"I worked hard getting ready for that game."

"Look, Wheels. Try to grasp the concept of Old Timer. The people interested in seeing you are guys your age, Joe Schlunks who paid to see a superstar, envying you getting paid big bucks to do every day what they would have given their lives to do once for free.

"These guys have gone as far as they'll ever go in their jobs or they're under big pressure to perform. They spend their free time in front of the TV with a beer. They've got bifocals, the passion's gone out of their marriages, their kids need braces or tennis lessons. They spend their holidays painting the house to save for their kids' college fund.

"When you run out on the field, Joe Schlunk doesn't want to say, 'God, old Wheels Wheeler looks just like he did in his playing days. Hasn't aged a day or put on a pound. He could probably still give these young guys a run for their money.' Joe Schlunk wants to know that you've aged, that you've put on weight, that you run like an old man, that he doesn't have to envy you any more.

"Joe Schlunk wants to be able to say, 'Hell, Wheels Wheeler may have been a great shortstop once, but I bet I could outrun him today.'

"What it comes down to, Wheels, is nobody likes to be embarrassed."

After he hung up the phone, Wheels said to Willene, "I'm not decrepit enough to be an Old Timer."

"Sure you are," said Willene. "It just takes training. You have to eat, drink lots of beer, and stop exercising."

Wheels smiled ruefully.

"It's like anything else," Willene went on. "Just work on it. Sleep on the ground for a few nights, ride in the rain without a slicker — you'll feel the arthritis stirring in no time."

There had been a shower earlier in the afternoon. The canyon was green, speckled with purple and yellow wildflowers, a chestnut colt frolicked on a nearby hill-side. Wheels wondered if the invitation to run for the state senate was still open.

He got up and walked slowly to the kitchen. He opened the fridge, eyed two pieces of apple pie and checked the freezer compartment, going eyeball to eyeball with a gal-lon tub of vanilla ice cream.

LUMPY DROBOT, DESIGNATED HITTER

If there's anything I hate more than my nickname, it's my manager, the guy who hung it on me.

Lumpy.

Lumpy Drobot, designated hitter.

"Lumpy runs with all the speed of water finding its own level," the manager is saying to a reporter. Then he guffaws, spraying spit. He was a shortstop in the Bigs for seven years, a powder-puff hitter, but feisty and mean-spirited — nicknamed the Surgeon because he spiked more runners sliding into second than anybody else in his era. That's why Cleveland kept him in the organization, made him a manager.

The rumor is that the day he spiked Johnny Mize twice, Mize waited for him under the grandstand, which explains why the Surgeon's nose is crooked and leans dangerously to the left.

He called me Lumpy even before I got hit-by-pitcher five times in five games. He called me Lumpy to motivate me. The Surgeon's theory is that if us players hate him enough, we'll play so well we'll get moved up to Triple-A and away to hell from him and our pitching coach, Beanball Monaghan, his drinking buddy.

Monaghan had been on his way to the Bigs when one night in Columbus his inside fastball ruptured the eardrum of the Yankees' number-one draft choice. The number-one draft choice never played again.

The Yankees bought Beanball Monaghan's contract from Oakland for a lot of money, demoted him to Double-A, and left him there to rot. They figured the best punishment was for him to get paid peanuts for being a star in Double-A. I could understand why he had the personality of a buzz-saw.

The Surgeon is sixty-seven years old. The reporter asks him why he's managing in the Double-A boonies when he's earned enough money and has had enough years in management that he could retire comfortably.

"Baseball kind of gets under your skin," he says, and guffaws spit past the reporter, who has learned not to stand in front of him during an interview. The reporter doesn't notice that the Surgeon is glancing sneakily at me all the time he's answering the question. Figures he's smart, the Surgeon does.

I've never been crazy about Drobot as a name, but I was born to it. It's a good Polish name, and I wouldn't change

it, even though in grade school the kids used to call me
Drobot the Robot. John is a nice neutral first name, and
Stanley isn't the worst second name I could have. In high
school some of the guys took to calling me Stan the Man,
after Musial, the most famous Polish baseball player of all,
and I certainly didn't mind that. My old man calls me
Stash, but only at home. He knows it used to embarrass
me at a game or when my friends were around. The old
man knew I had feelings.

But not my manager. The day I reported to Double-A
in Chattanooga, he looked me up and down and said,
"Drobot, I hear you run with all the speed of shit moving through a long dog."

After everybody stopped laughing, I said, "You hear
wrong. I'm not that fast," and I put out my hand to shake.
He ignored it.

"Listen, you lumpy son of a bitch," he said. "You better be one hell of a designated hitter, 'cause you sure
don't look fit for nothin' else." Then he guffawed, spraying brown spit.

The Surgeon was ahead of his time — he called me
Lumpy before I decided that getting hit-by-pitcher was
the way to make a name for myself. Before the miracle.

I am lumpy, I admit that. I'm 5'7", 190 pounds, and
never would have made it if it wasn't for the designated-
hitter rule. I can't cover much ground in the outfield,
and I'm too short to be a first baseman, but designated
hitter is something I'm good at. I've never hit below

.300 and I've got good power to all fields. I can stay with an outside pitch and slap it off — or over — the right-field wall. I love the feel of connecting solidly, knowing by the tingle that begins in my hands and runs up my arms that the ball will clear the fence, that I can stand and watch it go — that I don't have to chug around the bases like an overheated engine.

I hit .331 in my first two weeks with Chattanooga, but the Surgeon wasn't happy.

"Your on-base percentage is too low," he barked, the morning after I'd hit a game-winning homer in the bottom of the tenth. "You're short," he hollered, as if I didn't know that already. "A short, lumpy bastard like you should get hit-by-pitcher more often. When they come inside on you, don't back off. You've got bones like fucking plumbing pipes — you can take a shot. You're built like Don Baylor, only shorter and lumpier."

He sure knew how to make a young ballplayer feel good about himself. But the next time I came up and the pitcher came in on me I took it on the left bicep and trotted to first as the go-ahead run crossed the plate.

The Surgeon was right. Even though the ball had hit me solidly, the pain was hardly noticeable.

As I took a short lead off first, I remembered something I'd heard back in Legion ball: little guys have to prove they belong. Well, I thought, I'll always be a little guy, nothin' I can do about that. So I'm gonna do whatever I have to to prove that I belong. If that means gettin' hit, it means gettin' hit.

"Easiest RBI I ever got," I said to a reporter after the game. "Guess the skipper hollered 'Get a hit,' but I thought he said, 'Get hit!'"

"Lumpy here is doing what he has do to win ball-games," the Surgeon chimed in, clapping me hard on my bruised arm.

I'm going to hate my way right up to Triple-A and the Bigs.

The next morning my name appeared in the newspaper as John "Lumpy" Drobot. By the end of the week I was plain Lumpy, without quotation marks. My teammates started to call me Lumpy, too — "Get a hit, Lump," or "Bang it out there, Lumpy." And from the far corner of the bench I'd hear the Surgeon's high-pitched, piercing voice. "Get on base, you lumpy son of a bitch."

Over the next few weeks I became fearless. I'd crowd the plate, daring the pitcher to throw at me. If they tried to move me off the plate, I'd just turn into the pitch and take my base. If the pitch was outside I'd take it for a ball. If it was over the plate, I'd hammer it.

Even though I had a .300-plus batting average and lots of walks and had been hit-by-pitcher twelve times, the Surgeon still treated me like I smelled bad. Beanball Morgan ridiculed me at every opportunity, and I didn't have a friend on the team.

*   *   *

Everyone came to call me Lumpy. All except the Christians. They never called me Lumpy: they called me John. The Christians wouldn't say shit if their mouths were full of it. None of them had nicknames, just Dean, Robert, Alvin, Vernon — all guys who could slide into second base without getting their uniforms dirty.

They belonged to something called A*C*E, Athletes of Christian Endeavor. They prayed in one corner of the locker room before every game. They praised the Lord if they made the game-winning hit and said it was God's will if they butchered a double-play ball.

The Surgeon hated them at least as much as he hated me, maybe more. Though they never sulked, never talked back, never cursed, fought, got arrested or sneaked girls into their rooms, they didn't play any harder than they would have for any other manager. When the Surgeon ranted and raved and called one of them out for a mistake, he'd nod and smile but wouldn't play any differently the next game. To an Athlete of Christian Endeavor, the Surgeon was not the ultimate authority.

When the Christians would pray before a game the Surgeon and Beanball Monaghan would stare at them like they were exotic animals, then spit darkly on the locker-room floor and stalk off to the field, their cleats grinding on the cement.

One of the more fervent Athletes of Christian Endeavor was named Angel Correa — his first name was pronounced

Ann-hell — a sensational shortstop who spoke little English. Correa had the unfortunate habit of going around the clubhouse after a game, handing out three-colored religious tracts small as a credit card.

One night, after making the game-winning hit and being interviewed on the field after the game, I returned to the locker room just in time to see Beanball Monaghan take hold of Angel Correa by the gold chains around his neck.

"Hey, you habla the English there, Chico?"

Correa squeaked — could have been either yes or no.

"Don't matter, you'll get my drift." Monaghan raised Correa a foot off the floor and held him at arm's length. "Now I don't want you to take this personal, boy, and I sure wouldn't want you to consider this an infringement of your civil rights. Freedom of religion gives you the right to believe in whatever damn-fool thing you choose. However, personally, I feel that freedom of religion also encompasses freedom from religion."

Correa seemed to be developing a bluish tinge.

"So if y'all want to live long, die happy and not have your carcass nailed to the clubhouse wall, you'll never flash that literature around here again. The only time I want you to speak to me is if you need advice on throwing the curveball, which is unlikely seeing as how you're a shortstop. And" — he shook Correa from side to side a few times — "if you ever tell another reporter that it was the Lord's will that you popped up with the bases loaded I'll personally cut your life expectancy by about fifty-seven years."

Shaking Correa one more time, he set him down, and when he noticed the shortstop's knees buckle as his feet touched the floor, he smiled amiably and laid him carefully on the cool concrete.

When a player is a long way from home and when his manager and coach — who, at least in the minor leagues, are supposed to be father figures — hate him, he has to turn somewhere. Some of the players pounded the Bud, some had wives or girlfriends to turn to for comfort, to confide in, sometimes abuse. I didn't drink, I didn't have a girlfriend and I needed a friend; but friends were few and far between. Yet, there were the guys from A*C*E, just waiting, ready and willing as fly paper.

I reached out my hand, tentatively — and got stuck.

"I'm goin' to turn crazy if I don't talk to somebody," I said to a lanky outfielder named Robert Eager. "You guys seem to have a cozy little group. What do I have to do?"

Vernon Smith, a freckled, horse-faced third baseman with a slow Texas drawl, was standing behind me.

"Y'all don't have to do anything," said Smith. "Come along with us — we're headin' over to Perkin's Steak and Cake for a bite to eat."

"I could eat me a buffalo," said the fourth member of A*C*E, a relief pitcher with the unlikely name of Dean Breadfollow.

There was something too nice about them. It made me suspicious.

"You don't have to be afraid of us," said Robert Eager. "We're not much different than anybody else, except we believe our lives are guided by the Lord. We're merely vessels, listening vessels, and you obviously need someone to talk to."

"Good listen, man," said Angel Correa, who appeared from nowhere, half a dozen gold chains around his neck.

"I promise you, John, no one's going to try to convert you," said Smith. By calling me John he won me over.

And they kept their word. The five of us went to Perkin's and I laughed for the first time in weeks.

"What's bothering you?" Robert Eager asked. "What is it you really want to know?"

"I don't understand why I'm doing what I'm doing. Am I punishing myself by getting hit all the time? Am I just so ambitious that I'll do anything to succeed? Or . . ."

"We believe there is an answer to every question somewhere in the Scriptures." Vernon Smith held up his well-thumbed Bible. "Let's just do a little exploring together. We'll start in the obvious place, the Book of John."

That evening and the next we read through several chapters of John, but nothing seemed to apply.

It was Angel Correa who suggested Revelations. "Written by St. John the Evangelist," he said, pleased at his knowledge.

It was while reading the second chapter of Revelations that, like pieces of a puzzle, answers seemed to appear.

The second and third chapters of Revelations are John's letters to seven different churches. In each letter there are admonitions to those who had sinned but also rewards for "him who overcomes." I know this will sound odd, but we were all really tired after a long road trip and an extra-inning game. And as Vern Smith said, his face shining, "There's no accounting for fervor."

"'He that overcomes shall be arrayed in white garments, and I will not blot his name out of the book of life . . .'" read Robert Eager.

"Amen to that," shouted Correa.

"The home team uniform," said Dean Breadfollow.

It seemed logical to me. Our home uniforms were a blazing white.

"What is it you hate most about what's happening to you?" asked Vern Smith. It was the next evening and we were in Robert Eager's tiny basement room.

"My name," I said without hesitation. "Nobody likes to be called Lumpy."

"Then listen to this," said Vernon Smith. "Revelations 2:17. 'To him who overcomes I will give him a white stone, and in the stone a new name written, which no one knows except him who receives it.'"

"That's what I need," I said. "A new name."

"A white stone?" said Angel Correa.

"A baseball," said Robert Eager. "Hard as a stone when you get hit."

"Spalding?" suggested Vern Smith.

We all laughed uproariously, high as the players who drank too much or smoked dope.

"Lumpy Spalding," I said, doubled over with laughter.

"Spalding Drobot," said Robert Eager. "Sounds like something from a snooty prep school — Spalding Drobot, counselor-at-law."

"Or the hero of a romance novel. 'Spalding Drobot crushed Melanie's pale body in his tanned, muscular arms.'" We shrieked like grade schoolers.

"Actually, Rawlings makes the baseballs these days, in Haiti, on assembly lines manned by relatives of Papa Doc Duvalier," said Robert Eager.

Dean Breadfollow read again from chapter two, and I have to admit that in the heat of the moment it made sense. "'To him that overcomes I will give authority over nations.'"

"You'll become Commissioner of Baseball in Japan . . ."

". . . or Cuba . . ."

". . . or Haiti."

"They don't play baseball in Haiti. They play soccer. They'll make you Commissioner of Soccer for Haiti."

The emanation of the miracle began about the twentieth time I got hit-by-pitcher, when we were playing Knoxville. The fans roared as the pitch hit me. I was batting left-handed; the count was 2-0, and the pitch tailed in on me at the last second. I could have gotten out of the way but helped things along by almost stepping into it. I took the pitch full on the right bicep, as good a place as any to be hit.

But instead of the dull pain of ball bruising muscle, intimidating bone, it was as though the ball had exploded when it struck me. I could feel the shards, like tiny needles, spray to the farthest points in my body. My scalp prickled, my fingers tingled. My tongue felt as if I had bitten it.

I went down as the pitch hit me, but bounced to my feet quickly — ballplayers are taught to be macho about being hit. I stood stunned for several seconds, getting my bearings, trying to understand why I hurt all over instead of just at the point of impact.

My arm was sore and slightly swollen after the game. There was the beginning of a bruise, a small mottled area with pinpricks of red and blue. But instead of clearing up in a few days the way a bruise should have, it stayed sore. I could feel the soreness through my uniform. I could feel the swelling and feel my pulse throbbing in it.

In the shower, about the fifth day after being hit, I touched the swollen area with my fingertips, felt the puffiness on my upper arm. What I felt frightened me, but because of the steam in the shower I couldn't be certain. When I got to my room I checked the arm carefully. The skin was puffed up nearly an inch and the seams of a baseball were clearly visible on my skin.

The next time we played Knoxville, their catcher told me they never found the ball that hit me, the one that felt as though it disintegrated and entered my body.

"I thought it just rolled to the backstop," I said.

"Since there was nobody on base I didn't pay much attention," said the catcher. "But when I looked around it was nowhere to be seen. But the ump slapped another ball into my glove and the game went on."

"You don't have to become a freak by getting hit by pitches. You can make the grade on your ability," said Robert Eager. We were sitting in what the other players and management called the Christers' Corner of the locker room.

By now the lump was so big it distended the loose sleeve of my uniform. "I want to show you something," I said. "I want you to tell me what it is." I gently pushed up my sleeve so they could see.

They stared, their fingers suspended in midair as they almost touched it.

"It's a miracle," said Robert Eager.

"'And in the stone a new name written,'" said Dean Breadfollow.

"You never gonna be Lumpy to nobody no more once you find out your new name," said Angel Correa.

Everyone in the locker room gathered round.

"What the fuck are you guys doing? You got a whore in there?" asked Beanball Monaghan, pushing his way into the circle.

The ball was recognizable under the translucent skin of my bicep, as if it was covered by the whiteness of surgical-glove rubber.

"Hey, Skip, come look at this," Beanball Monaghan called to the Surgeon. "Fucking Drobot has baseball in his blood." Everyone except me and the members of A*C*E were laughing.

"Have you been to the doctor?" asked an outfielder.

I shook my head.

"And he ain't gonna," snarled the Surgeon. "We need the baseballs." He guffawed like a fool.

Robert Eager got a tiny knife from the trainer. He poured rubbing alcohol over the blade, then touched it gently to the distended skin of my upper arm. I felt a pinprick of pain, less than a mosquito bite, and the pale skin peeled back, leaving a glistening, mucous-coated baseball — radiant, luminous, white.

The ball balanced for a second, then dropped to the floor. We all stood gaping at it.

"What a bunch of pansies you are," said Beanball Monaghan. He picked up the ball, wiped the wet glaze up and down the front of his uniform. "I used to deliver calves back in Oklahoma." He tossed the ball back and forth, hand to hand.

"Let me see it," I said.

Monaghan held it up to the light, turned it slowly. "Regulation baseball," he said. "Perfect condition. Something mighty fishy here." He turned it some more.

"Hey, it's Lumpy's baby," said one of the players. "Give it over to him to hold."

"Maybe he wants to nurse it."

"Yeah, you got resin in your tits there, Lumpy?"

"At least the lumpy son of a bitch has got tits. He won't have to bottle-feed it," said the Surgeon, spraying tobacco juice.

Monaghan picked up another baseball off a bench. He tossed both in the air, then flipped them back and forth.

"Don't do that," I said.

Monaghan bounced both balls off the wall, catching them on the rebound. He dribbled first one then the other, like miniature basketballs. Then, with an evil laugh, he tossed them into a wire basket of batting-practice balls.

"You're young and healthy," sad Monaghan. "You'll produce other offspring." Everyone except those from A*C*E roared with laughter.

I rubbed my hand over the spots where I had been hit by pitches in recent weeks. I could feel the slight puffiness of the skin in each area — I was indeed going to produce more baseballs. But surely the first one would have my new name in it.

The game doesn't start till 7:30 tonight, but I'm at the park before noon.

"That's a fine-looking equipment bag," the old man at the players' gate says to me.

"Carried a few bats home for sanding and taping."

He doesn't notice that the bag says "McCulloch" in big red letters all down one side, and I'm sure not going to point it out to him.

Just as I figured, I'm alone in the ballpark — it's damp down under the grandstand, smells moldy the way a grave must. It takes me only a couple of concentrated shoves to break open the door to the equipment room. The snapping of wood sounded like gunshots to me; but there's only me here, and the old man is way off at the players' gate in left field.

A sick little pimple of a light bulb swings back and forth on a dark cord, casting eerie black shadows. The bases are stacked up like pancakes against one wall. There are bats all over the place — some in racks, some in boxes, some bumping my ankles like huge matches. I breathe in their varnishy smell and the leather odor of the baseballs. In the corner are a couple of buckets of "mud" so the umpires can rub the shine off new baseballs before each game.

There must be three hundred used balls, all loose, like a cache of eggs, in what looks like a child's playpen with chicken-wire sides. There are also a couple of wire baskets half-full of batting-practice balls.

I fire up the McCulloch. The odor of burning oil tickles my nose. One of those baseballs is mine: conceived, brought to term, birthed. It will take me a few tries to get used to the saw, but I have all afternoon. I pick up a ball covered with grass stains and bat marks to practice on. I carry it to a waist-high shelf, hold it gingerly with my left hand, approach it with the saw.

It is easier to split than I imagined. I reach for another ball. One of them has my new name in it.

THE
DIXON
CORNBELT
LEAGUE

"Mike, I think I've found the perfect place for you to play," my agent says. His name is Justin Birdsong, and we've never met. He signed me up because a year ago I looked like a top prospect for the Bigs. The last time I heard from him was a few days after the college draft — where I wasn't picked up. He said that in spite of the lack of interest in me, he thought he could find me a job in minor-league baseball.

Not being drafted was a particular disappointment, though not unexpected; the Expos had drafted me fourth in my junior year, and I turned down a sizable signing bonus because I wanted to finish my degree, and because I felt I needed another year of experience. Well, I got the experience. If I had been injured, then I could have had something on which to blame my decline. My average fell from .331 to .270, my stolen bases from forty to nineteen, and I was caught stealing nine times. My play at second base, which has always been just adequate, remained that way.

I don't blame the pros for not drafting me, but I also feel that if I get in a solid year of minor-league ball, they'll be willing to have another look.

After the draft *Baseball America* called me the best-looking second baseman not drafted. "In practice, Mike Houle is as good as anyone who's ever played the game. Perhaps with experience he'll get a second look from big-league scouts."

"I can get you a contract with a team in Iowa," Justin Birdsong says. "League representative called this morning. They've got openings for all kinds of players, but they are especially interested in you. You'd be with a semi-pro club in the Dixon Cornbelt League. They play good-quality baseball, close to Double-A, they assure me. They also tell me that the big-league scouts make regular stops."

"It doesn't look as if I have much choice," I say. "Teams aren't exactly burning up the phone wires to either me or you, and everything I get in the mail is addressed to Occupant."

"That's the spirit," says Justin B. "I'll tell them you accept. They'll wire you travel money. You're to report to Grand Mound, Iowa, day after tomorrow. Oh, one other thing. Since the Dixon Cornbelt League is unaffiliated, all the teams are self-supporting. What will happen is you'll get a base salary, but one of the sponsoring merchants will give you a job in the mornings. You'll have your afternoons free for practice, and you play in the evenings."

The salary he names isn't enough to pay room and board, and I tell him so.

"Forgot to mention, you get free room and board with a local family. I only take commission on your baseball pay. The league representative said that since you're a business major the local insurance office will take you mornings. You'll do fine."

"It doesn't look as if I have much choice," I repeat. "I'll be there."

At the Cedar Rapids Airport, I am met by a large, hearty man named Emmett Powell. The weather is hot, humid for so early in the year. Powell is in shirt sleeves, his gray suit coat over his arm. He might have been an athlete thirty years ago. Now, his thinning hair is combed straight back off a high, ruddy forehead. His belly swells comfortably over his belt.

"Well, Mike," he says, pumping my hand, "I'm sure you're gonna enjoy your summer in Grand Mound. And, no, before you ask, the town wasn't named for a pitching mound, though there was a town over near Iowa City called Big Inning, and it was named for baseball."

We make our way to his car. His wife, a pleasant, innocent-looking woman, is there. A high-school-age girl and a docile brown-and-white spaniel are in the back seat. The wife is Marge, the daughter Tracy Ellen, the dog Sarge.

"We'll be putting you up this summer," Emmett Powell says. "In a small town like ours there's competition for who gets to house the ballplayers. Among families with marriageable daughters it gets downright fierce," and he laughs good-naturedly.

"Oh, Dad," says Tracy Ellen, exasperation in her voice. She is a pale blonde with a few freckles across the bridge of her nose.

"Emmett, you behave yourself," says Marge. "Don't want to frighten this boy away."

"I just hope Mike likes cherry pie," says Emmett. "One thing we do in Grand Mound is eat well, and nobody bakes a better cherry pie than Tracy Ellen. Unless of course it's her mother."

"Think you'll be able to stand all this wholesomeness?" asks Tracy Ellen.

"It'll be a change," I say. "My mom died when I was eight. My dad, my older brother and me have been baching it ever since."

"That's what we heard," says Emmett, and I wonder, briefly, where. But I suppose whoever scouted me checked into my background, too.

"What about my job?" I ask.

"Oh, didn't I mention? You'll be working for me. I'm the independent insurance agent in Grand Mound. Got me a little office on Main Street, but do most of my business from the house. Folks just drop by when the spirit moves them. It's certainly not the fast lane, but we live well. I'm planning to retire at sixty-two, just ten years from now. It will be a fine business for an enterprising . . ."

"Emmett, the boy hasn't even seen Grand Mound yet. Don't be trying to sell him your business. You'll have to forgive him, Mike," Mrs. Powell says, turning around to face me, "Emmett and his friends are so enthusiastic about small-town life. They're worried that the small towns are going to disappear in a generation or two."

"Did you know, Mike," Emmett picks right up, "Iowa has more small towns for its size and population than any other state. They say it has a town about every mile-and-a-half on every secondary highway. But the farms are getting larger and the farmers fewer in number. When the farmers go, the small towns die. But I guess we won't have to worry for a few years. Grand Mound is one of the few towns to show an increase in population. And I believe having a team in the Dixon Cornbelt League is a prime reason. You'd be surprised at how many of our players decide to settle down here."

The Powells live in a two-story, white frame house on a tree-lined street. My room is on the second floor, large and bright with a huge double bed and polished hardwood floors.

They do eat well — roast pork and potatoes, three vegetables, iced tea, cherry pie. They force seconds on me, offer thirds, insist on a late-evening snack of pie and ice cream, repeatedly point out that I am free to raid the refrigerator at any time.

"What other teams are in the league?" I ask Emmett as I accept another piece of pie and ice cream from Tracy Ellen. "My agent didn't know, or didn't tell me much."

"Not likely that you've ever heard of the teams, all small towns that sit in a row along Highway 30. There's Mount Vernon, Lisbon, Mechanicsville, Wheatland, Grand Mound, Clarence, and DeWitt."

"That's seven teams," I say. "Makes for a difficult schedule."

"Makes for three games every night of the summer," says Emmett jovially. "DeWitt's the biggest town, almost five thousand people, Mount Vernon's next with four thousand, only us and Wheatland have less than a thousand. Big towns use some local talent. We had to import our whole team at first, but this year you're one of only five new players. Most of the team has settled down in Grand Mound, several have married local girls."

His eyes move to Tracy Ellen, who is sitting beside him on the sofa, balancing her plate on her knee. She is wearing pastel-pink shorts and top. Her feet are tiny, her shoes the same pink as her clothes.

"How long has the Dixon Cornbelt League operated? I took a quick glance at the Sporting News but couldn't find out anything about it. And how long has Grand Mound had a team?"

THE DIXON
CORNBELT LEAGUE

"Oh, the league has been around for years and years. We're unaffiliated, outside of organized baseball, which is why the *Sporting News* doesn't write us up. Grand Mound has had a team for, oh, several years. You'll like the other players, most of them are college boys like yourself."

"I want to show you something," Emmett says later in the evening. I am sitting on the porch swing watching fireflies quivering in the tall honeysuckle. The night is silent, the heat seems touchable, velvety. Emmett picks his way down the three steps to the driveway, beckons to me in the instant before he becomes just another shadow amidst the moonlight-gilded leaves.

I get in the passenger side of the car and Emmett drives the few blocks to Highway 30, not turning on the lights until we are at least a block from the house. The highway is a ribbon of blackness winding between equally black fields — planting is just finished for the season.

"What you're gonna see," says Emmett, "are small-town baseball fields. The other teams do their practicing at night. In fact, there are exhibition games on down the line a ways. If you hadn't had such a long flight, and if it wasn't your first night here, we could've scouted the opposition. Every second town we pass will have a stadium lit up like Times Square. From a distance some of them look like fire on the ocean . . ." and he trails off, unable to find the right words.

He is right, for there are no words to convey what we see.

Suddenly, around a sweeping turn, like a burst of fireworks, sits the ballpark. Or, as we roll along, it blooms out of the sensitive blue-black night like a giant marigold. We glimpse the emerald grass, perhaps a flash of white uniform, before passing the park, the lights suddenly behind us as if we are driving into ink.

The next town appears subdued, a twinkle of streetlight the only illumination. Usually we can pick out the empty ballpark, huddled beside the highway like a huge, sleeping animal curled against the night. We press on, watching the horizon for the golden aura of another ballpark, another night game.

In the morning, after a breakfast offering more variety than most cafés, we head for the office, Marge and Tracy Ellen waving goodbye from the porch as Emmett backs the car out.

Powell Real Estate and Insurance occupies half of a small, yellow-painted building on Main Street. The other half houses a barber shop. The office consists of three very old wooden desks buried under mounds of papers, three three-drawer filing cabinets, and a table holding a coffee maker. The building faces east and the window is tinted blue to keep the room cooler.

Emmett assigns me the smallest desk, explains that a part-time secretary comes in three half-days a week to do most of the clerical work and bookkeeping. Fifteen minutes after we arrive there are five people in the office, all there to appraise the new second baseman.

After another fifteen minutes Emmett hangs a small, well-worn sign on the glass of the front door: back in 5 minutes. Then we all make our way across the street to the Doll House Café, where, I suspect, I meet half the population of Grand Mound and vicinity before we head home for lunch. The constantly changing crowd — a farmer in bib overalls or a townsman in shirt sleeves — comes in, sits at our table for a few minutes, exchanges greetings with people at the other tables, and moves on.

The café owner, a large, jolly woman named Mrs. Nesbitt, offers me breakfast, then forces pie and milk on me, tries to feed me seconds.

What puzzles me is that every person who drops by promises to be at our practice, which is set for 2:00 P.M.

And they are. The Grand Mound team is called the Greenshirts, and our uniforms are a beautiful enamel-white with kelly-green trim, numbers, and names. Our sweatshirts and socks are the same blazing green.

The field is picture perfect, lovingly tended. The fence at the foul lines is 298 feet, the centerfield wall 350 feet away. As we begin our warmups the stands are filling, just as if for a game. Behind the main grandstand the concessions are open, dispensing hot dogs, ice cream, and soda.

The groundskeeper, a stoop-shouldered man named Jeremy, comes around to shake hands with each player, says if we have any suggestions as to how he can improve the playing field, just to let him know.

There must be over eight hundred people at the practice, about three-quarters of what the stands can hold. We enjoy a routine practice and workout: calisthenics, wind sprints, stretching exercises, batting and fielding practice. The squad is larger than I would have anticipated, over thirty players with a preponderance of pitchers.

The manager is a surprise, a name I know. Gene Walston is a slim, gray-haired man with a complexion like concrete. Walston had been a third-base coach in the Bigs for many years, had the nickname "Suicide" Walston from his propensity for waving runners around third no matter how slim their chance of scoring. He even got to manage the final fifty games of a season after the manager had a heart attack. But the team blew a five-game lead and lost their division. The next season Walston was gone — over five years ago now. It never occurred to me to wonder what had become of him.

It looks as if I am going to have competition. There is another second baseman, a year or two older than me, a better fielder but he doesn't appear to be as fast on the bases. I can't tell from batting practice what kind of hitter he is.

"We'll play our first intersquad game tomorrow night," the manager says, as practice is breaking up.

It is after that first intersquad game, played to a full house, that I begin to suspect something unusual is

going on. We are two distinct squads, half in home uniform, half in road uniform, green with white trim. But
immediately the game is over, a round, freckle-faced
man shakes my hand.

"I'm Dilly Eastwick, the sports editor," he says, his
small hand damp in mine. "I cover every Greenshirt
game myself. Now, Mike, I want you to know I really
appreciated your play this evening. Why, you danced
like Baryshnikov all around second base. And that backhanded stop you made in the seventh inning was one of
the best plays I've ever seen."

"Thank you very much, Mr. Eastwick," I say.

"It was a perfect pleasure to watch you play." His
eyes twinkle, and his round moon face beams.

The line about me dancing like Baryshnikov appears in
the next edition of *The Grand Mound Leader*. Later in the
week, he compares my throws to first from deep behind
second and the right-field grass to a gunboat firing across
the prow of a suspect ship. In the following issue he tags
me with a nickname. "Mike 'Gunboat' Houle," the story
says, "effortlessly handled six chances in the field, and
turned the pivot flawlessly on three double plays."

One cannot help but be pleased with press like that.

The next week, Dilly, as he insists all the players call
him, writes about the catcher for the Green squad, Bill
Baker, a boy from Mississippi who arrived in Grand
Mound the same day I did. "He fires clotheslines to second base," Dilly Eastwick writes, "so straight and true

that the flight path remains marked in the air for innings. You could hang the family wash on a throw by 'Clothesline' Baker."

And so it goes. Dilly Eastwick eventually writes up every newcomer to the team. The returning players all have nicknames, courtesy of Dilly Eastwick, I assume. The townspeople address us by our nicknames when we pass on the street.

"When do they start making the cuts?" I ask a player who is starting his third season with the Greenshirts.

"Oh, not for a few days yet."

"But there are so many players," I insist. "Two full squads."

"Don't fret," he says. "They carry a large roster."

"I can't believe how pushy my parents are," says Tracy Ellen, coming to sit beside me on the porch swing. At supper Emmett, for about the tenth meal in a row, praised her cooking to the skies. "They're so obvious."

"They mean well," I say.

The moon hangs heavy, the color of papaya. The leaves of the mountain ash in the front yard are flickering with moonlight.

"If it'll take some of the pressure off, I have a boyfriend," says Tracy Ellen. "He doesn't play baseball."

I feel the tiniest tinge of sadness.

"They're pushing us together so hard I pretty well have to," she goes on. "But I think it would be nice if we could be friends. My brothers are a lot older, went off to college — one lives in New York, one in Chicago. They have families."

"Having you for a friend would be great," I say. "I've never had a sister. It'll be fun."

"Maybe you can ask Dad to stop trying to marry us off?"

"I'll try to be tactful," I say.

I don't succeed.

"Tracy Ellen and I have made an agreement," I say, on the way to work the next morning. "We're going to be friends, not sweethearts. So you can stop promoting a romance."

Emmett, all innocence, looks at me over the top of his glasses.

"Besides, Tracy Ellen tells me she has a boyfriend."

"A boy from Mechanicsville," says Emmett, his voice full of disapproval. "Built like a Clydesdale, and I might be doing a disservice to the horse to compare their intelligence."

"Sure you aren't just being a protective father?"

"His name is Shag Wilson. He chews snuff. He drives a customized half-ton with tractor tires about eight feet tall."

"You've made your point."

Something is not right here in Grand Mound, but I can't put my finger on it. I have been here a month now and I have never been happier. The Dixon Cornbelt League opener is in a few days. We play an intersquad game every night, hold an informal practice in the afternoon, work in the morning. We fraternize little. Our families are there after every game, we head home with them. I am playing better than ever in my life. I can't wait for a big-league scout to discover me — I'll bet the way I'm playing I could jump straight to Triple-A. But when I think of that, even when I think of the Dixon Cornbelt League opening, my back tightens, and the lump of live anxiety that has followed me all my playing days reappears in my belly. I hoped it had gone away, but it was only lurking out in the night.

When I think of the pressure from the fans, from the manager, from myself . . . the voices of all my coaches blend like crows scrapping: close your shoulders, level your swing, even your stance, hit on the ground, take an outside pitch to the opposite field, cover the bag, turn the pivot, on your toes, glove on the ground, back-up the base, take the cut-off, a walking lead. With all the snappish voices whirling about me I freeze, mind and body.

I remember jolting awake during the college season. I was standing at my position when I should have been covering first on a sacrifice play. The first baseman charged, the pitcher fielded the bunt — and had no one to throw to. The fans jeered, the pitcher slammed the ball into his glove, glowering at me. The manager, in the dusk of the dugout, spit in my direction. I want to become invisible. I don't want to play professionally — I only want to play for fun.

THE DIXON
CORNBELT LEAGUE

*   *   *

I don't like Dilly Eastwick. For all his sincerity there is
something sneaky about him, not exactly evil but
furtive, always looking over his shoulder. Even while he
is smiling and shaking my hand his eyes are somewhere
in the corner of the room.

After practice I drop in at the stone-pillared Grand
Mound Library, one of the original Carnegie endow-
ments Emmett told me proudly.

"Well, Gunboat, how can I help you?" says Mrs.
Thoman, a sturdy woman in a blue crêpe dress.

"I'd like to see *The Grand Mound Leader* for the current
month but from, say, three and four years ago," I say. I
find it embarrassing to be called by my nickname, especially by this cross-looking, matronly librarian, but I also know
she never misses a game. She always sits directly behind
first base, clutching a white-on-green pennant. The green-
on-white pennant holders tend to sit on the third-base side.

"Are you certain you want to do that?" she asks, in
what, for her, is a motherly way.

"I'm a great fan of Dilly Eastwick," I say. "I just want
to read some of his past columns."

Mrs. Thoman turns away, leaving me on the buckling,
brown linoleum, the library smell of dry paper and var-
nish heavy in the air. She returns with an armload of
papers and deposits them on a table.

As I read, she makes several phone calls, but I can't
make out any of her whispered conversations.

What I find immediately confirms my suspicions. In a column four years ago, Dilly wrote, ". . . last night our second baseman, Lew 'Gunboat' Driscoll, danced like Baryshnikov around second base." A day later he wrote about the new catcher, ". . . August Marsh threw a clothesline to second base in the seventh inning to nail a runner. The flight path was so straight and true that it remained marked in the air for innings." Dilly closed by saying, "August 'Clothesline' Marsh is going to have an outstanding season for the Greenshirts."

I don't say anything. Twice I suggest to other players that after our regular intersquad game we drive to one of the other towns, look over some of our competition. The players glance at me strangely, each declining. Their families are waiting for them.

Then Emmett announces that our opening game has been postponed. We were supposed to play Mechanicsville.

"Some of their college players haven't arrived yet," Emmett says. "We'll make the games up later in the summer, wouldn't want to take advantage of them when they're short-handed."

"We don't need a league," I say. "We get a full house for every intersquad game."

I think I hear somebody laugh.

When the postponement is announced, Gil Morgenstern, a pretty good left-handed-hitting third baseman, has a fierce argument, first with the third-base coach, then with the manager, and eventually with Emmett, who then makes his way into the manager's office, glancing apologetically over his shoulder. The result is that Gil Morgenstern packs his equipment and is driven to Cedar Rapids to catch a plane home to New York.

"Emmett, Grand Mound really doesn't have a team in the Dixon Cornbelt League, do they?" I ask that evening. "Be honest with me." We are sitting on the porch swing, the sky is still indigo, a few fireflies jiggle among the honeysuckle.

"Well now . . ."

"My agent believed he'd found me a genuine amateur league, where the big-league scouts would be looking in . . ."

"Well now, Mike, your agent's way out in California, and what he doesn't know about Iowa would fill a book or two. We may have exaggerated a bit, stretched the truth, if you will . . ."

"Like lying about Grand Mound being a member of the league?"

"Now, Mike, we have the league's word that if a team drops out, or if a franchise fails, Grand Mound gets the first opportunity to enter a team."

"For how many years?"

"Pardon?"

"How long have you been waiting?"

"Folks here are set in their ways, Mike. They don't change much."

"How long?"

"We've . . . we've been in our present situation since just after World War Two."

"But how could you do this to me, to the other players?" I'm trying to stay calm,. be reasonable. "Do you realize how unfair you are? You're ruining our chances of playing professional baseball just so you can entertain the local people, while convincing us to live here permanently."

"It's not like that at all, Mike. You're smart, and I like you a lot. In fact I'd be proud to have you as a son-in-law . . ."

"If things aren't the way I described, how do you see them?"

"Mike, what kind of a ballplayer were you in college?"

"Pretty good. You know my record."

"What did you do when the pressure was on, Mike?"

The force of it is like a knife twisting in my chest.

"I . . . well . . ."

"What did you do when things got tough, Mike?"

"I choked. The year I had to impress the scouts, I choked."

"We know. And we understand."

"Then, everyone . . . ?"

"Including the manager."

"'Suicide' Walston. Of course . . . Do the other play-ers know?"

"Yes. And I've taken a little razzing from the boys down at the Doll House Café. Did you believe in Santa Claus and the Tooth Fairy for a long time, too?"

"As a matter of fact, I did. I didn't want to believe there was anything odd going on here. Everything is so perfect . . . Is that why Morgenstern left?"

"He was a denier, Mike. Claimed he'd never choked in his life. Didn't believe a word we told him. He'll be better off back in New York. Not happier, but better off."

"Is there something magical going on here?"

"Magical? No."

"But a team that isn't a team?"

"Mike, the people who originally got the idea were years ahead of their time. They saw the future, Mike, saw that the small towns were going to die, dry up and blow away like fall leaves. And they asked, how can we keep our town together? We can't stop our young people from going off to the cities, but maybe we could bring some young folks here. If we made life attractive for them, they would stay here, marry into the community, keep the faith, so to speak.

"We saw baseball as the key to luring young men here, but we didn't have a team in the Dixon Cornbelt League, and no real chance of getting one. We brought in talented players, but when they found out there was no league, nothing but intersquad games, they were gone like a flock of startled birds. Then someone hit on the idea of scouting players who didn't come through in the clutch. We had seen hundreds of them, some of us had been there ourselves — pretty fair ballplayers till the crunch came.

"In Grand Mound we gave those players a place to play baseball where they'd never have a chance to choke. The first few years were pretty rough, but you know, Mike, deep in his heart, every choker knows it. The odd one won't admit it, but for most it's such a relief to know the pressure's off that they make a real effort to fit right in here in Grand Mound."

"Everyone on the squad knows but me?"

"Some are slower to catch on than others, Mike. I think it's been over ten years since any player spilled the beans. We only bring in four or five players a season now, and soon, we hope, the whole squad will return intact."

"And Marge and Tracy Ellen? They know everything?"

"Can't live around Grand Mound for long without knowing. Marge and I have been married twenty-seven years, and even back then I had to compete with a ballplayer who was courting her. That was a real dilemma. If she married the ballplayer, Grand Mound gained a citizen. They'd have been a lot happier if I went off to Iowa City or Ames and brought back a wife, but they let nature take its course, and happily, Marge chose me."

"And you chose me for Tracy Ellen?"

"I scouted you, Mike. Actually the whole family scouted you. The three of us flew down to U. C. Davis, watched seven home games. We even sat at the next table to you in a restaurant called the Blue . . . something-or-other."

"Blue Parrot."

"Right. You were with a dark-haired girl and another couple. You ordered roast beef and cherry pie à la mode."

"Tracy Ellen scouted me, too?"

"You were her choice for second base."

"What about the boyfriend with the truck, Shag Wilson?"

"Nice boy. If you check the files you'll find he got his truck insurance at a whopping discount."

"That's devious."

"Mike, are you happy?"

I consider for a few seconds before nodding.

"Sleep on it, son. I honestly think you could catch on with a Triple-A ballclub, and if your heart's set on giving it a try, no one in Grand Mound will stand in your way."

I lay awake for a long time. Tracy Ellen was out, and I mentally tracked every vehicle that turned off the highway until the customized truck rumbled down the street and turned sharply into the driveway. Their goodbyes were short.

When she comes in I am waiting on the landing. "You don't have to do that any more," I say. "Unless you want to."

"You know?"

"Yes."

"I was afraid you'd leave, like Morgenstern. You're not going to leave, are you? You're not mad?"

"I can't be mad at people who mean well, who know me better than I know myself. There's only one thing that can make me leave, and that's if you want to keep up this brother-sister arrangement."

I take her in my arms, tentatively at first, for she is light and fragile against me, but there is a tenacity in the way she holds the hair at the back of my neck as she presses her mouth to mine. We tiptoe down the stairs and out onto the honeysuckle-drenched porch.

We sit on the swing, Tracy Ellen with her legs curled under her, an arm around me, her head on my shoulder, her pale hair turned silver by the moon.

"Memorial Day is coming up," says Tracy Ellen.

"We play a doubleheader."

Then, "When did you know you were going to stay?"

"I think I decided a long time ago. There's something about the way you wave goodbye in the mornings, as if you'll really miss me, that breaks my heart."